CRACKING Love

Emily King

BELLA
B O O K S
2018

Bella Books, Inc.
P.O. Box 10543
Tallahassee, FL 32302

Printed in the United States of America on acid-free paper.

First Bella Books Edition 2018

Editor: Lauren Humphries-Brooks
Cover Designer: Judith Fellows

ISBN: 978-1-59493-573-2

About the Author

Emily King grew up in one of the many farming towns in California's central valley. She attended pharmacy school in southern California and practiced pharmacy for a number of years. She has also worked in farming and now writes fiction. In her spare time, she enjoys cooking with the bounty of food found at the local farmers' market, reading, getting in a good workout, and catering to the whims of her cat.

Acknowledgment

A thank you to Bella Books, and a thank you to my readers.

CHAPTER ONE

Janet Webber squinted against the setting sun as she emerged from the sliding doors of the baggage claim area at the Sacramento International Airport. She caught sight of a shuttle van to the parking lots, but its doors were closing. She was *not* going to miss it. She had already waited for one too many shuttles this leg of her business trip, and she wasn't going to let this one pass her and be stuck waiting for the next one. She unlooped her laptop bag from her wheeled carry-on suitcase, slung the bag over her shoulder with her purse, and sprinted in her pumps toward the curb with the wheels of her carry-on squealing. She all but flung herself through the shuttle's doors.

"I would've waited, you know," the driver said, her brown eyes amused.

"Thanks," Janet said a little breathlessly as she wrangled her luggage aboard the van full of other passengers.

"Here, let me get that for you," the driver said, getting out of her seat.

Janet surrendered her luggage, and the driver turned to place it on the rack. The driver's chinos tightened nicely over her shapely rear as she bent down. Her shoulders worked beneath her uniform polo shirt as she finessed the laptop bag into one space and the carry-on suitcase into another. Impulsively, Janet asked, "Are you a new shuttle driver? I only recently moved to the area, but I fly most weeks so I recognize a lot of the drivers. I'm Janet."

The driver straightened and turned around with a smile. "Yes, I started about a month ago. I'm Tina." She reached out her hand for Janet to shake. Smiling, Janet shook it.

The other passengers had taken the few seats in back, leaving Janet to stand and grab one of the handholds in the front of the shuttle. As Tina began the drive to the parking lots, Janet's gaze drifted to her hands on the wheel. Her gaze stopped on the thick band of a wedding ring on Tina's finger. Figures—with a body like that, she's already taken. Janet gave a little sigh that she hoped was drowned out by the sound of the van's engine.

"What brought you to Sacramento?" Tina asked with a glance back at Janet.

"Oh, I live here now. In Danforth, actually. I came from Connecticut about six months ago for a new job."

"What do you do?"

"I'm Western Regional Account Manager for Rockland Healthcare Solutions. We contract with hospitals to provide pharmacy services. I oversee the start-up of the new accounts and maintain the existing accounts."

"So you're a pharmacist then?"

"Yes."

"Interesting. I didn't know pharmacists did that kind of thing." Tina glanced at her again. "This is a new job for me too. Or a new route, anyway. I was a shuttle driver before, but not at the airport. I drove a downtown shuttle route for public transit in Los Angeles."

"What brought you to Sacramento?"

"My partner's job. She works in the capitol building." Tina cast an assessing glance at Janet.

Janet had the impression that Tina was trying to gauge her reaction to the use of the word "partner." Tina probably encountered any number of intolerant passengers each day. Tina might also have assumed that she was straight. People tended to assume that about Janet, and she wished they wouldn't since it all too often resulted in her getting asked out on dates by men rather than women. Janet was wearing her typical business attire, a dark blue suit with a pale blouse and a thin gold necklace. She had styled, blond hair that fell slightly below her shoulders, and she wore a light application of makeup that she knew brought out her blue eyes. Janet wasn't sure if her business persona was somehow conveying heterosexuality to Tina, but at the next opportunity she would disabuse Tina of any such notion.

"What does your partner do in the capitol building?" Janet asked.

"She works for Assembly Member Dan Fernandez from the Los Angeles district. We moved up here so that she could be an aide in his capitol office. She used to work with him in the mayor's office in Los Angeles, where he was chief of staff and she was an office assistant."

"Sounds like a nice career move."

"Yes. She was really happy when he ran for state assembly after the mayor's term was up. She's excited about getting experience working in the capitol. I'm excited for her too. I can work anywhere, so it was no big deal to move."

As the shuttle neared the first parking lot, passengers began standing and moving toward the luggage rack. A few people grabbed their luggage and exited the moment the shuttle stopped. Tina got up and assisted the others with their luggage. "How do you like your new job?" she asked as she resumed driving.

Janet was inclined to give a generic answer to someone she had just met, but Tina had been sharing with her, so she decided to answer more fully. "Well, it has its challenges. The travel is tougher than I thought it would be. I fly most weeks of the month, so I'm on the road a few days each week. And I'm still getting the hang of dealing with some of the characters I meet. Depending on the hospital I fly to and the people I encounter there, a few days can seem like a really long time."

"Oh?" Tina asked.

"Yeah. This last account that I was just at was one of those. It was a new account, so I had meetings with hospital administration and department heads as usual, but there was a physician there who kept trying to involve himself in everything. He's the head of a couple of committees and apparently felt the need to insert himself into practically every one of our meetings. He took up everyone's time. I got the impression the others put up with him because he gets a lot of patient referrals for his specialty area that brings in a lot of money."

"He sounds like a piece of work."

"He was. He even invited himself out to lunch with us and hit on me."

"No," Tina said, disbelief in her voice.

"Yes, I'm afraid so. The others seemed used to his behavior, but it took a lot of effort for me to stay polite. Even if I weren't gay, why would I be interested in such an egomaniac?"

Tina turned her head at that. Janet smiled at her. *That's right, I'm a lesbian too.*

Tina stopped at the next parking lot to let more passengers out. After helping some of the people with their luggage, she returned to her seat and continued driving. Tina cast more glances at Janet, and seemed to be assessing her once again.

Janet waited, wondering what she was thinking.

"My partner—her name is Susan—and I are having a housewarming party this Saturday," Tina finally said. "You should come. It sounds like you could use some fun after your trip. We're having a lot of friends over—friends from Los Angeles and a few people we've met here."

Janet was pleasantly surprised at the invitation but unsure whether to accept. "Oh, thank you, but I wouldn't want to intrude. I wouldn't know anyone but you."

"Well, that's the idea, to meet new people." Obviously trying to encourage Janet, she added, "Some of the women are single."

"Well…" Janet considered. But really, there was not much to consider. It would be nice to go to a housewarming party full of women.

"Give me your phone number before you get out of the shuttle, and I'll text you the time and address."

"Okay." Janet nodded. "Sounds good."

When the shuttle arrived at Janet's parking lot, Janet collected her bags from the now nearly empty rack. She handed Tina a business card with her cell phone number on it, and said goodbye.

Janet drove the half hour from the airport to her apartment in Danforth. She passed through the corporate business parks on the outskirts of Sacramento. Traffic was tolerable right now in this state capitol of about half a million people, but she preferred living in her smaller city of Danforth. The freeway afforded her a view of Sacramento's buildings in the distance beneath a layer of fluffy white clouds. The sunset bathed everything in a golden-pink glow, and the waters of the surrounding marshlands glimmered.

Janet parked in her space in the carport of her apartment complex. She stopped by her mailbox to grab three days' worth of accumulated mail and then climbed the stairs with her luggage to her second-floor unit. She unlocked the door, flipped on the lights, set down her bags, and shut the door against the noise of street traffic.

Returning home to her empty apartment was not a high point of Janet's travels. Janet was beginning to think that leaving Connecticut for this new job that she wasn't particularly fond of so far had been a mistake. She missed her friends, her old co-workers, and her family, even if her parents were very set in their ways and did not approve of her "lesbian lifestyle," as they put it. That housewarming party of Tina's was going to be something to look forward to.

Janet set her mail on the kitchen counter. The light on her answering machine was blinking, so she hit play. A couple of hang-ups, probably telemarketers. A political robocall. A message from her friend, Katie, who also worked for Rockland Healthcare Solutions. When Janet was Director of Pharmacy at Fulton Hospital, her job before this one, Katie had worked for her as the Pharmacy Manager. Now Katie was Director of

Pharmacy. It was good to hear from her. Janet worried that their friendship was going to drift apart now that they lived on the opposite ends of the country. Janet thought Katie was handling the pressures of the directorship well, especially since she was a little over halfway into a second pregnancy.

Janet's stomach growled. She opened her refrigerator, but all that was inside was the leftover remains of a meal too old to eat, some cheese, and a package of aging carrots. She hadn't had a chance to shop before leaving town. She shut the refrigerator and sighed. She didn't want to leave after having just arrived but didn't want to call for a pizza delivery, either. She deliberated only a little more and then picked up her purse to head out for dinner.

At the Danforth Bistro, Janet slid onto one of the comfy stools at the bar, letting the soft yellow lighting and pleasant wood tones of the popular restaurant and bar relax her.

"Did you come in for your veggie burger?" Debbie the bartender grinned at her.

Janet nodded. "I sure did." Janet was not a vegetarian, but she loved the bistro's veggie burger. The patty was a wonderful, savory creation that involved too many components for her to identify, but she knew from the menu description that there were walnuts and mushrooms in it. She could only guess at the rest of the ingredients but was almost certain that there was some secret flavoring like soy sauce or miso paste. Whatever it was, it was delicious and was served with a slice of melted mozzarella cheese on a buttered, toasted bun.

"I just opened a new bottle of the house pinot noir. Would you like a glass of that with your burger?" Debbie asked.

"Sure."

Debbie retrieved the bottle of wine, poured a glass, and placed it before Janet.

"Thanks." Janet relaxed on the padded barstool and sipped her wine. She listened to the hum of conversations around her and the gentle clatter of silverware on plates.

Debbie arrived with Janet's veggie burger. Janet took a bite, and savored its deep, rich flavor. Or, at least she tried to. She didn't know if it was her imagination, but the veggie burger tasted a little off this evening. She regarded it. It looked the same. She took another bite. But it didn't taste the same.

Debbie was watching her. "Is your burger okay?"

"That's just it. It's 'okay.' It's usually delicious. Did the chef change something?"

Debbie nodded and pursed her lips. "You're not the only customer to notice. The chef didn't change anything, but our new owner did. He told Robert, the manager, to cut costs, so Robert eliminated our local suppliers and now just gets everything from a regional wholesaler. For the burger, we used to get our walnuts from a local grower, Lawrence Farms."

"Wow, who knew that could make so much difference?"

"I know. I've been hearing complaints all week. I told Robert, but he thinks people will get used to the change."

Janet picked up her burger to continue eating, but without much enthusiasm. "What happened to the previous owner?"

"He wanted to retire from the restaurant business, so he sold. Did you notice the salad is a little different too?"

Janet poked at the accompanying salad on the plate. The lettuce didn't seem as fresh and delicate, and the toppings looked a little pale and dry. "Now that you mention it, it does look a little different."

Debbie nodded. "The lettuce and tomatoes used to come from Lawrence Farms, just like the walnuts, but now they come from our wholesaler with the rest of our supplies. The tomatoes come pre-sliced in a container, and the carrots come pre-shredded in a big bag."

Janet was taken aback at these drastic changes. "Doesn't that bother the chef?"

"Yeah, he's bothered, but he wants to keep his job. The new owner was pretty firm about cutting costs." Debbie sighed. "None of us want to rock the boat."

"Is it going to save that much money?" Janet asked.

"I don't think so. I don't think the cost is really much different, considering the big difference in quality." Debbie shook her head. "I think the main thing is that Robert wants to show the new owner that he's doing something. I guess he hopes that with our volume it will make some difference."

"Well, if the taste of the food suffers, I doubt this way of doing things will work."

Debbie nodded. "The restaurant has been busy as usual, but these changes only just started. Even though we have a good crowd tonight, I'm worried."

"I agree. I think I'll say something about my food to the manager. Do you think you will get a moment to call him over here?"

"I can—" Debbie stopped short and looked to the restaurant entrance.

Janet followed her gaze and saw a woman who was in discussion with the hostess.

"That's the owner of Lawrence Farms right there, Gail Lawrence." Debbie motioned with her head in the direction of the woman. "I've only ever seen her here before business hours. I wonder what she's doing here now."

Janet took in the woman's appearance. Even from her seat at the bar across the room, Janet could see that Gail Lawrence was an attractive woman. She had dark eyes framed by dark eyebrows, high cheekbones, and a head of short brown hair. She stood tall and straight as she spoke with the hostess. Janet liked tall women, because she was tall herself at five-foot-eight.

The hostess picked up her phone and spoke briefly into it. Gail Lawrence's eyes tracked to the back of the restaurant, where a man had emerged from a doorway with a resigned expression on his face. Gail strode purposefully toward him.

"That's Robert, the manager," Debbie said. "It looks like Gail came to see him."

"It doesn't look like he wants to see her. She seems upset. It's probably about him changing suppliers, don't you think?"

Debbie nodded. "Probably."

Janet continued to watch from afar. There was frustrated gesticulating from Gail, head-shaking and crossed arms from Robert, and frowning from both of them. There was an intensity about Gail that drew Janet in and made her care as much as

Gail clearly did about the topic of discussion with Robert, which had to be the changes at the restaurant. Although Gail was a stranger, Janet was bothered that Gail was upset and that Robert appeared unreceptive to what was being said.

Abruptly, Gail turned and strode from the restaurant. Janet frowned and looked at Debbie. "I don't think that conversation went well at all," Janet said. Debbie snorted in agreement. "Never mind what I said about talking to the manager. I'm pretty sure now is not a good time for that."

The next morning, Janet sat down at her desk with a mug of coffee and logged on to the Rockland Healthcare Solutions website. Being able to work from home some of the time was an aspect of her new job that she enjoyed. She spent the morning completing reports and finishing other work related to her new account. Most of her reports could be filed online, but she would have to stop by the post office to mail some documents to company headquarters in Boston.

She checked her corporate email account. Elaine, secretary to Aaron Robson, the Senior Account Director who was Janet's boss, had emailed the flight, hotel, and rental car reservations for her assignment next week. The rest of the emails were various regulatory and administrative questions from the directors of pharmacy at her accounts, and she typed out responses.

Janet's phone buzzed with a notification. She looked at the display and smiled. Tina had texted the time and address of her housewarming party on Saturday, with a note that food would be provided so not to bring anything. Janet was looking forward to seeing Tina again and to meeting her partner, Susan. She was also looking forward to meeting some single women. With her work schedule, meeting other single lesbians wasn't easy to do. Janet realized that she needed to get a housewarming present for Tina and Susan and made a mental note to buy it while she was out running the rest of her errands.

Running errands took most of the day. By the time Janet got home with her groceries, she had worked up quite an appetite, especially as one of her errands had included a trip to the gym for a workout on the elliptical trainer. It always felt good to move her body after a previous day spent in a cramped airplane seat. She set her bag of groceries on the kitchen counter and began filling her refrigerator with food, setting some items aside for dinner. After so many meals out this week due to being on the road and then coming back to a nearly empty refrigerator, it was going to be nice to cook and eat dinner at home.

She intended to make pasta with spring vegetables, one of many favorite dishes that her grandma had taught her to cook. She put a pot of water on the stove to boil while she prepared the ingredients. As she picked up a bundle of asparagus from the counter, the printing on the band around the bundle caught her eye. *Lawrence Farms*. Was that Lawrence Farms, as in Gail Lawrence? It must be. The asparagus was beautiful, just like the other vegetables at the Danforth Bistro had been until management changed suppliers.

Janet recalled the physical attractiveness of Gail herself and felt a little thrill run through her body. She wished the conversation between Gail and Robert had gone better, not only for Gail's sake, but also so that Gail might have stayed longer at the restaurant, maybe even wandered over into the bar where they might have met.

Janet brought her attention back to cooking dinner. She removed the band from the asparagus and cut the asparagus into bite-size lengths. After she was done blanching the asparagus and some peas, she boiled fettuccine noodles while she made the pasta's yummy garlic and lemon cream sauce. When the noodles were ready, she drained them and added them to the skillet containing the sauce, along with the blanched vegetables and some salt and pepper. She tossed it all gently together while it heated through, then transferred it to a dish and grated some Parmesan cheese over it. She prepared a plate for herself and sat down to eat. She took a bite. The asparagus was perfect, and even more flavorful than the kind she used to get at the farmers' market in Connecticut. Management at the Danforth Bistro was crazy to stop using Gail Lawrence's produce.

CHAPTER TWO

Janet turned onto Tina's street. If the numerous parked cars lining both sides of the street were any indication, there was going to be quite a crowd of women at Tina's party. All the better to finally meet some local lesbians. Spotting an open parking space along the curb, Janet pulled to a stop a few houses down from the address Tina had given her. She grabbed her housewarming gift and got out of the car.

Tina's house was pleasant pale green stucco with white trim. The simple act of visiting a house reminded Janet of her own house back in Fulton, Connecticut, which was on the market now. She missed her house. Getting used to living in an apartment again was a little difficult. Even pared down ahead of the move to California, Janet's belongings did not all fit in her one-bedroom apartment. As soon as her house sold, she planned to buy a house here, get the remainder of her things out of storage, and get herself out of her small, not to mention noisy, apartment. That is, if this job out here started to agree with her better.

Janet walked up the little walkway leading to the house and knocked on the door.

"Hi," said the smiling blond woman who opened the door. She had an open, friendly face that made Janet like her immediately.

"Hi, I'm Janet. Tina invited me?"

"Oh, yes, hi! Tina told me all about you. I'm Susan, Tina's partner." She gave Janet a quick hug. "Come in."

"Did I hear my name?" Tina asked. She appeared in the entryway and put her arm around Susan.

"Hi, Tina." Janet gave her a smile, happy to see her new friend again.

"Hi, Janet." Tina reached for Janet's hand and gave it a friendly shake. "I'm glad you could make it."

"Thank you for inviting me. This is a housewarming present for you both." Janet handed Susan a one-pound bag of coffee beans with a bow on top. She had gotten it at a local coffee house while she had been running errands the other day.

"Thank you," Susan said, taking the gift. "That's so thoughtful. We both drink coffee, so I'm sure we'll enjoy this."

Tina nodded. "Now come on in, and I'll introduce you."

Janet tried to keep up with the names of everyone she was meeting. Many of the women Tina introduced her to worked in downtown Los Angeles, where Tina had driven the shuttle route for public transit. They held a variety of jobs, from bus mechanic to department store sales clerk to librarian to security guard. There were also women who used to work in the mayor's office with Susan in Los Angeles. All of the women from Los Angeles were interesting, but Janet was more pleased to meet some locals from Tina's and Susan's new workplaces in Sacramento. Everyone seemed friendly and made her feel welcome, and Janet was already enjoying herself. Even if she didn't come away with a date, maybe she would come away with some new friends in Sacramento and Danforth.

After a break in conversation, she went over to a table that was set up with hors d'oeuvres. Picking up a plate from a stack, she began selecting from the assortment of food. A hand touched her upper arm and a voice said, "Hey, I heard you're a pharmacist. Does that mean you can get me some drugs?"

Janet stepped away and turned her head to see who would be asking such a ridiculous question. A redheaded woman whom she had not yet met stood there. Janet assessed the expression on the woman's lightly freckled face. Her expression was hard to read, and Janet couldn't tell if she was joking or serious. Janet set down her plate. "No, it doesn't work that way. Pharmacists can't just hand out drugs to people."

The woman opened her mouth, but before she could say anything more, another woman angled herself between them and extended her hand for Janet to shake. "Hi, I'm Gail. How about I get you a drink to go with your snacks?"

Grateful for the interruption but keeping a wary eye on the redheaded woman who had asked for drugs, Janet absently clasped the proffered hand. The hand was pleasantly warm, the handshake firm. The name Gail suddenly registered with Janet. Janet turned and found herself looking into the handsome face of Gail Lawrence. Janet smiled as she gazed into the brown eyes above strong cheekbones that she had only previously seen from afar in the Danforth Bistro.

Out of the corner of her eye, Janet noticed the redheaded woman wander away and nearly gave a sigh of relief.

Gail had released Janet's hand and was looking at her with an expectant smile.

Belatedly, Janet said, "Hi, I'm Janet. And yes, I would like a drink."

"Beer or wine? Or soda or water?"

"I'll try the red wine."

Gail turned to pour two glasses of wine from one of the open bottles. Janet let her gaze drop, taking in the curve of Gail's hips in her dark slacks and her trim waistline.

Gail turned back to Janet and handed her one of the glasses of red wine.

Janet hoped she hadn't been caught staring. "Thank you," Janet said, accepting the glass. "And thank you for that a moment ago."

"Was it that obvious that I was trying to interrupt? I heard that strange question, but I was trying to seem oblivious to the conversation when I interrupted so as not to seem too rude." Gail shrugged good-naturedly.

Janet chuckled and took a sip of her wine. "Who was that woman, anyway? Do you know?"

"No, I don't know who she is. I haven't seen her with Tina or Susan before."

"Well, I guess it doesn't matter." Janet smiled at Gail. "You know, I should mention that I actually know your name already."

"Oh?" Gail smiled at her.

Janet liked having Gail smile at her. "Yes, I saw you the other night at the Danforth Bistro. I was eating dinner at the bar. The bartender Debbie told me your name and that you own Lawrence Farms. We had just been talking about your walnuts and produce when you walked in."

"Really?" Gail seemed pleasantly surprised.

"Yes. I had just gotten back into town. I thought I would go have one of my favorite meals, their veggie burger made with what Debbie told me are your walnuts. Or, I guess I should say that used to be made with your walnuts. Debbie told me that the restaurant changed suppliers. I saw you talk to the manager. It looked like you might have been upset."

Gail nodded and gave a sigh. "I was. I drove over to the restaurant after work to talk to Robert in person because he hadn't been returning my calls about the change in suppliers. That's what I was upset about. I wanted to know the reason for the change and to make sure he wasn't dissatisfied, and of course to ask if he would reconsider."

"What did he say?"

"He said he wasn't dissatisfied at all, which I was glad to hear, but he was unreceptive otherwise. He told me that the new owner is only interested in the bottom line. Robert doesn't want to cut staff, so he's changing suppliers and contracts on most everything." Gail shook her head. "I told him that if he starts getting all of the restaurant's produce from some central distributor, customers are going to notice."

Janet nodded.

"Local food is freshest," Gail said firmly. "Something from a warehouse simply cannot be as fresh or as good-tasting as something just picked from my farm or from another local farm."

"I definitely found that out last night with my meal. If the taste difference was any indication, I think his changes are going to backfire."

Gail nodded. "The previous owner believed in supporting local farms. I'm sad to see that end with this owner. And I'm disappointed to lose the contract, but I'm confident that I can make up the sales elsewhere."

"That's good." A couple of other guests approached the food and drink tables. Gail gently touched Janet's arm and guided her aside. Janet appreciated the chivalry of the gesture, especially as they were now standing closer.

Gail smiled at her and took a sip of wine.

Janet wanted to know more about Gail. "How do you know Tina and Susan?"

"We all worked in downtown Los Angeles. I used to take Tina's shuttle on my lunch hour. So did Susan. That's actually how she and Tina met."

"Oh, so you're from Los Angeles too? Tina told me that she and Susan moved here for Susan's job. How did you end up in Sacramento?"

Gail paused before replying, long enough for Janet to notice a slight frown flit across her forehead and a tightness develop along her jawline.

"I just...moved back. I'm from Sacramento originally. Danforth, actually." Gail's voice sounded tight. She cleared her throat. "Six years ago, I guess it was, that I moved back," she added faintly. Her eyes had taken on a distant look.

Janet had also wanted to know what Gail's job had been in Los Angeles, but now she was hesitant to ask. "It must be nice to have your friends nearby again," she ventured.

"Yes," Gail replied absently.

Janet regarded her with curiosity.

"Gail?" Janet and Gail both turned their heads at the sound of Susan's voice from the kitchen doorway. Susan gave them a smile. "Gail, could you come here a moment? I think Tina's outside, and I need a little help with a platter."

"Sure." Gail turned back to Janet. "Would you excuse me?"

"Of course," Janet answered with a smile. "Maybe we can chat more later."

Gail returned her smile. "I'd like that."

Glad to see Gail's good humor restored, Janet wondered if she had imagined the brief change in her demeanor.

Gail entered the kitchen, where she found Susan preparing a tray of food at the counter.

"I'm loading up this tray to take outside so that Tina can start grilling," Susan said. "It's going to be too heavy for me to maneuver with through the crowd. Can you take it outside to her?"

"Sure, I can do that." Gail set her wineglass on the counter.

"Let me just add a few more things." As Susan continued to prepare the platter, she glanced over at Gail with a teasing look on her face. "I saw you swoop in and save Janet from Eileen at the hors d'oeuvres table."

"'Swoop'?" Gail asked with a small laugh. Susan sometimes had a flair for the dramatic.

"It looked like swooping to me," Susan said with a grin. She paused. "Janet looked a little annoyed by whatever Eileen was saying to her."

"Yeah, she looked uncomfortable. I overheard—Eileen, did you say?—ask Janet if she could get her some drugs."

"What!"

"Yeah, do you believe that? I hope she was kidding. Who is she?"

"Eileen is Lisa's ex-girlfriend, apparently the kind of ex that keeps hanging around. I think you met Lisa this evening. She works in the cafeteria in the capitol building. Lisa told me that Eileen invited herself along tonight to try to meet other women.

I don't know Lisa or Eileen very well, but I don't think they're into drugs, so hopefully Eileen really was kidding."

"Yeah, because asking a pharmacist for drugs isn't a good idea for a pickup line."

Susan snorted and shook her head. "I know, right? I wonder if she tries to pick up bank tellers by asking them if they can get her some money?"

"Yeah, really." Gail shook her head. She recalled the look on Janet's face as Janet had tried to interpret Eileen's intentions. "I don't think Janet would have needed any help handling Eileen, but I thought an interruption might be nice."

"I can see a lot from the kitchen, and it definitely looked to me like she thought it was nice." Susan had returned to her teasing tone.

Gail smiled but shrugged, feeling suddenly self-conscious.

"Yeah, I saw her check out your butt when you turned to get her a glass of wine."

Gail's smile broadened.

"And don't think I didn't see you checking her out, too."

Gail didn't deny it. Janet was pretty and had a great figure. Gail had enjoyed the feel of Janet's soft hand in her own, and it was hard not to be drawn in by her expressive blue eyes. On top of that, she seemed intelligent and pleasant.

"Janet's new to the area, and I don't think she's going to be single for long," Susan said.

Gail sighed. She knew Susan meant well with her prodding—Susan always did—but she wished that her friend would let her move at her own pace with Janet. Gail fiddled with her wineglass, sliding it in little circles on the counter.

Susan finished preparing the platter, casting glances at Gail. "Gail? Is something the matter?"

Gail let out a heavy breath. "Seeing all these faces from Los Angeles reminds me of Christine."

"Christine? Christine again?"

Gail jumped slightly at the exasperation in Susan's tone.

Susan put her hands on her hips. "Christine's cheating was years ago. Not everyone is a cheater."

"I know," Gail said, trying not to sound sullen, "but it's hard not to be reminded of her at times. Like tonight. Seeing all of our friends from Los Angeles is great, but it also takes me back to some painful times."

"Christine is out of the picture, so there's no need to think of her. If you ever want something that lasts any length of time again, you are going to have to forget about the pain."

"I know, and I'm trying not to be reminded of her and to put her behind me, but I don't like being hurt."

"Well, who does?" Susan shrugged. "But it happens. You have to stop worrying that a relationship is going to end badly before you even give it a chance to start."

Chastened, Gail nodded. It was reasonable advice. She wished that it were easy to follow.

Janet wandered into the living room. Women had crowded onto the couch and were watching women's college basketball on TV. Judging from their shouts and banter, they were very into it. Janet wasn't that much of a basketball fan, so she continued walking to the patio door, through which she could see several women gathered at a long patio table with their hors d'oeuvres and drinks. Their good-natured chatter and ribbing of each other gave Janet the impression that they were a group of long-time friends. Everyone here was friendly, and Janet was sure she'd be welcome to join in with the group, but she wanted to be available to chat with Gail when Gail came out of the kitchen. She had yet to find out if Gail was single.

Janet glanced back toward the kitchen. No sign of Gail yet. She sighed and walked out onto the patio, where she spotted Tina off to one side at a barbeque. Tina was applying lighter fluid to a mound of charcoal. She struck a match and lit the pile of coals. Janet loved eating barbecued food but barbecuing wasn't allowed on the small balcony attached to her apartment, so this meal was going to be a treat. As Tina looked up at her approach, Janet gestured to the barbecue. "You're a traditionalist, I see."

Tina laughed. "Yes, I like the taste from a charcoal barbecue."

"I do too. What are we having?"

"Just burgers and hot dogs and veggie versions of both. I'm going to keep it simple today with the crowd."

"Sounds really good." Janet continued to make small talk with Tina as the coals heated and she watched for Gail.

Movement of two figures at the sliding glass door drew Janet's attention. Gail and Susan. Janet couldn't help but let her eyes move over Gail's tall and trim but curvy body. Gail strode confidently forward as she carried an awkward and heavy-looking tray full of food for the grill. As Gail handled the tray, Janet admired the movement of the muscles in her forearms below her rolled-up sleeves. Gail's attention was on Janet in return, and Janet felt all of her senses awakening in a very pleasant way under the appreciative gaze of Gail's brown eyes.

Tina indicated a place on a table next to the barbecue for Gail to set the tray. "Right here is fine, Gail, thanks." Tina turned to Susan, who had followed behind Gail with a glass of wine in each hand. "This platter looks great, honey. The coals are almost ready." Tina spread the pile of coals around a bit.

Susan handed one of the glasses of wine that she was carrying to Gail and went to stand by Tina. From Susan's glance at Janet and then at Gail, Janet had the impression that Susan had moved in part to give Janet the opportunity to stand closer to Gail. Had Gail and Susan talked about her in the kitchen? Maybe Gail was indeed single. Janet stepped into the vacated space and was rewarded with a smile from Gail.

Tina arranged the hamburger patties and hot dogs on one section of the grill and then the veggie versions on another section.

The veggie burgers reminded Janet of her dinner the previous night. "Gail and I were talking earlier about the food at the Danforth Bistro," Janet told Tina and Susan. "Did you know the restaurant has a new owner and the manager dropped Gail as a supplier?"

"What? No," Tina and Susan said in unison. They looked at Gail with concern. "What happened?" Susan asked.

Gail filled them in, gesticulating with her hands while she talked. Janet remembered the feel of her hand in Gail's earlier in the evening. Gail had grasped her hand firmly but gently, and Janet had felt a few calluses, which told her that Gail probably was actively involved in the work at her farm. Getting dropped by the restaurant had to hurt, even if Gail had said she could make up the sales elsewhere.

Tina and Susan were both frowning after hearing Gail recount her conversation with Robert. Janet was glad that her new friends were as affronted by the events at the restaurant as she was. "I ate there after the changes," Janet told them both. "It's very different."

"If it's going to be different, then I'd better tell my boss Dan," Susan said. "He has a lot of catering done by that restaurant. He may want to have catering done by someplace else now."

"I like the way you think," Janet said. She turned to Gail. "Are there other restaurants that feature your produce?"

"Sure, several," Gail answered.

Janet turned back to Susan. "Do you think you could get your boss to switch to another restaurant that supports local farmers like Gail?"

"Yes, I'm sure I could. That's a good idea." Susan turned to Gail. "Can you give me a list so that I'll be able to suggest some to him?"

Gail nodded. "I'd be glad to." She smiled at Janet.

Janet smiled back, enjoying the satisfied feeling that trying to correct the indignity of Gail being so callously dropped by the restaurant's management brought her.

The aroma of the cooking food began to draw the rest of the women outside. Tina put the cooked burgers and hot dogs on a fresh platter. Everyone made their choices of food and applied fixings to their burgers or dressed their hot dogs and then found places to sit and eat. Janet sat with Gail, Susan, and Tina near a group of their friends from Los Angeles. She joined the conversation occasionally but mostly enjoyed listening as the friends caught up with one another, wanting to learn more about this dynamic group of women. But it was hard not to be distracted by Gail. Her figure certainly was flattered by that button-down shirt with the rolled-up sleeves. As Janet's eyes lingered on the swell of Gail's breasts, she realized that she had lost track of the conversation. Feeling a little warm, Janet took a breath, mentally shook herself, and refocused her attention on the discussion around her.

A woman named Trudy was talking. "I just bought a new pair of turquoise boots! They're much prettier than my old boots. They have white and gold stitching."

"Have you worn them yet?" asked one of the women at the table.

"No, I'm going to wear them tomorrow night."

Janet wondered what tomorrow night was. It must have shown on her face, because Trudy said, "We're going dancing. Want to come with us?"

"Dancing?" Janet repeated.

"Yes, we're staying for the whole weekend before we drive back to Los Angeles on Monday. We came not just for this housewarming party but to all go line dancing together again with Tina and Susan. Gail too." She swept her arm in the direction of the three women. "We don't all get to dance together anymore, not since they moved up here. It's going to be fun!"

Line dancing. Janet didn't know much about it. Tina and Susan were smiling at Trudy. So was Gail, but her smile looked a little forced. She no longer had the casual posture of the moment before and was now sitting up with her hands tensely clasped in her lap.

"How about it? Want to come with us?" Trudy asked again.

As Janet was about to reply, Eileen came to stand near the group. Janet hoped she wasn't going to intrude with another ridiculous question.

Janet turned to her attention back to Trudy. "I –"

"Some of us that live around here are going too. I can take you," Eileen interrupted.

Janet wasn't about to go anywhere with this intrusive Eileen person. Janet looked over to Gail, wishing that she'd had been the one to offer to take her, but Gail had a distant look in her eyes, just as she had earlier in the house when the conversation had also turned toward Los Angeles. Janet addressed her answer to Trudy and the rest of the group, rather than to Eileen. She hoped Eileen would get the hint that she wasn't interested in her so that she didn't have to spell it out. "Thanks for inviting me to go with all of you. It sounds like fun. But I don't know how to line dance, and even if I did know how to line dance, I can't go. I have an early flight on Monday."

"You do? Where are you flying?" Trudy asked.

"Seattle," Janet answered.

"Ooh, fun!"

"Well…not really," Janet replied, hating to dampen Trudy's enthusiasm. "It's for work."

"I thought you were a pharmacist," Eileen interrupted.

"I am," Janet said.

"Oh." Eileen gave a confused frown.

Janet didn't feel like explaining her job to Eileen, but she realized that Trudy and the other women listening to the conversation might have the same question. "I'm a manager," Janet said to the group. "I'm going there to check on some things in a pharmacy."

Several of the women nodded their heads in understanding. Janet thought again about her early flight departure time tomorrow and couldn't help but be frustrated. Her schedule was already going to make her miss an opportunity to hang out with her new friends. She wanted to know more about the line dancing that these women all used to do in Los Angeles, especially if line dancing was something that Gail liked to do. "Trudy, tell me more about line dancing. What is it like?"

Trudy leaned forward eagerly. "Well, it's basically dancing in a group to the same steps, in rows. There are all kinds of dances to do."

Janet waited for Trudy to say more, but she seemed at a loss.

"Maybe we should just show you," Trudy said. She turned to her friends. "Should we show her, ladies?"

There was a chorus of enthusiastic responses, and several of the women stood up. A few of the women complained about not having worn their boots tonight. Janet didn't know what to make of that. Tina and Susan began moving chairs out of the way. Gail stood up to help, apparently having snapped out of whatever thoughts were occupying her. Other women stood and moved to the lawn to make more room on the patio. Soon there was a clear space on the patio.

Trudy stood in front of her friends. "Ladies? We don't have our boots, but I think we can all manage to do Slappin' Leather anyway, right?"

The women answered in the affirmative and lined themselves up in rows. Tina and Susan joined in but Gail stayed off to the side after helping with the last of the chairs. Janet was a little disappointed. She wanted to see Gail dance.

"On my count. Five, six, seven, eight!" Trudy said.

As one, the women moved their heels forward to tap twice and then toes back to tap twice. There was more heel and toe tapping and then they brought their bent right legs up behind them to slap their shoes with their left hands. The women were smiling, and a few let out whoops of enjoyment as they danced. So far, the dance did look fun and not overly difficult. There was more leg bending and shoe slapping. Janet had a pretty good idea of why the dance was called Slappin' Leather. As one, the group turned and did some other footwork while stepping in a line to the right. They all clapped once and reversed direction to the left, clapped once again and then stepped backward in a wide, wiggling walk. The women came forward and all jumped their feet together in a stomp, and the dance ended.

Janet applauded, as did others. The dancers bowed or curtsied, laughing, and some exchanged high-fives.

Janet laughed. "That looks like a lot of fun! You say you normally wear boots to do this?"

"Yes," Trudy said as she caught her breath. "Some of the places even require boots." Trudy glanced at the group. "But even if boots weren't required, it's fun to dress up in western wear! Am I right, ladies?"

The women laughed out their agreement.

Susan turned to Janet. "A lot of the steps are easier in boots. The dances involve things like sliding, scuffing, and turning, and you need a shoe without tread for that."

"It's safer in boots too," someone chimed in. "I have a friend who wore athletic shoes and turned her ankle."

Janet drew back in surprise. She didn't normally think of dancing as being dangerous.

"I wore loafers once, and my foot kept slipping out," Tina said.

Gail walked over to join the group from where she had been standing and watching during the dance. She had pushed her memories away as best she could so that she could enjoy watching her friends dance. She had also taken the opportunity to observe Janet during the dancing demonstration. Gail loved how Janet's face had lit up as she watched the impromptu dance. Janet had looked beautiful.

"You didn't want to dance?" Janet asked.

Gail shrugged. "I'm a little rusty. I've only been line dancing a few times since leaving Los Angeles."

"Are you going with everyone tomorrow night?"

"Yes."

"Where do you go dancing?"

Tina was first to answer. "The Pink Stallion, a gay bar here in Sacramento. They have line dancing every Sunday night. It draws a nice, mixed crowd."

"I wish I could go tomorrow with everyone. I'd like to try it."

Gail felt the need to do something about the look of disappointment clouding Janet's features. "I can take you some other time if you'd like to go."

Janet looked at her and brightened instantly. "Yes, I would like that."

Gail smiled.

"I don't have any boots, though," Janet said.

"Boots aren't completely necessary at The Pink Stallion. You can wear other shoes, especially if you just want to try it out."

"From what everyone said, it sounds a lot better and safer to do the steps in boots. You'll be wearing boots, won't you?"

Gail nodded.

"I want to wear boots too. I don't mind shopping for some, because I can probably wear them other places around here too."

"I can take you boot shopping," Susan said. "I know the owner of The Sacramento Western Barn. They have a great selection of boots. The owner was one of Dan's campaign contributors, and he offered discounts to all of Dan's staff. We can go there, and I can see if I can get you a discount too."

"That would be great," Janet said.

Gail began moving chairs back in place, and a few other women came to help her. Guests gathered their empty plates and glasses to take inside. Women came up to Tina and Susan to thank them for the party and to say goodbye. Gail finished arranging the chairs, then turned to see Janet standing nearby, chatting with one of the stragglers. Janet was the first woman who had drawn her interest in a long time for something more than the occasional one-night stands that she had. She wanted to make plans to take Janet dancing, and she didn't want her friends to interfere. "Can I walk you to your car?"

"Yes." Janet smiled warmly. "Just let me say goodbye to Tina and Susan."

A few minutes later, Gail and Janet exited the house together. It was dark out now, but the porch light provided some illumination. "I'm parked just a few houses down," Janet said as they walked down the driveway.

Now that Gail had Janet to herself, she was suddenly nervous. She hadn't asked anyone out in a long time. And anything involving dancing usually caused thoughts of Christine to creep in, and they were doing so now.

"I'm glad Tina and Susan invited me to this party," Janet said softly.

"I'm glad too." Gail liked Janet's intimate tone of voice, liked that it was for her.

Janet stopped in the glow cast by a streetlight and gestured to a Toyota Camry. "This is me."

Gail looked at the car. "This is you?"

"Yes." Janet looked at her. "You sound surprised."

"I guess I thought you'd have a luxury car." Realizing how rude her comment must have sounded, Gail mentally kicked herself. "I'm sorry. I don't know why I said that." *I am really not myself tonight.*

Janet regarded her silently through narrowed eyes.

Gail tried to backpedal further. "Not that a Camry is not luxurious. I just thought as a pharmacist you'd have something higher end."

Janet frowned. "I happen to like my car."

Oh boy, I think I'm making this worse.

Janet crossed her arms. "So, was rescuing me from that rude woman at the hors d'oeuvres table a mistake, then?"

"What? What do you mean?" Gail asked.

"You know, at the start of the party. You heard I was a pharmacist, so you thought you'd latch onto me, that I'd be rich, have a luxury car?" Janet was gesturing a little wildly with her arms.

"No, that's not—"

"If you're hoping for luxury, pharmacists aren't the ticket. Sorry to disappoint."

Gail raised her hands in placation. "I didn't mean to suggest anything. I'm sorry." She made to touch Janet's shoulder in reassurance, but Janet backed up. Gail stopped.

Janet was shaking her head. "Please tell me you're not a gold digger, just after people for their cars and other possessions."

"A gold digger? Me? No, of course not!" Why would Janet think that of her from a simple observation about the car?

"Then why do you care what kind of car I drive?"

"I don't!" Gail realized that she had become loud. This wasn't at all how she had wanted things to go. She took a breath and let it out. "I don't know what I was saying. And I don't understand why you're so upset. I do just fine for myself. I'm not a gold digger."

Janet regarded her for a moment, frowning. "I had an ex who was a gold digger. It's a sore point. I don't need that again. No one wants to attract someone who is just after cars or money."

"I wasn't—"

Janet raised her hands. "It was a long time ago, when I was in college. I guess she thought that when I graduated from pharmacy school and started practicing, the money would start rolling in. When she found out that was the not case, she lost interest and started dating a physician. I don't know how I didn't realize she had some kind of master plan. It would have prevented a big waste of a relationship."

"I'm sorry," Gail said. "I see why my comment upset you."

Janet let out a breath and nodded.

Gail looked her in the eyes. "I'm not a gold digger."

"Okay."

She didn't look entirely convinced but she at least seemed calmer. Gail hoped Janet wasn't always this high-strung. She smiled tentatively. She wanted to restore Janet's good spirits. She thought back to Janet's comment about the hors d'oeuvres table. "So, I 'rescued' you in there, huh?" she ventured. She was relieved when Janet's blue eyes softened and the corner of Janet's mouth quirked up in a small smile.

"Maybe," Janet said.

"Let's say I did. And I assure you, my intentions were good."

Janet nodded. She reached into her purse, ostensibly to search for her car keys. While she rummaged, she cast a distracted glance at Gail. "So, where'd you park your car?"

Sensing Janet's returning good mood and hoping she wouldn't wreck it, Gail waited a beat and then asked in a knowing voice, "You're wondering what kind of car I drive?"

Janet looked up quickly, exasperation plain on her face.

Gail gave her a teasing smile.

Janet's exasperation disappeared. She shook her head and chuckled. "Very funny," she muttered.

Pleased with herself, Gail nudged Janet's shoulder. "And anyway, what makes you think it's a car?"

Janet glanced at up at her again, and Gail was further pleased to see a full smile.

Having found her car keys, Janet fidgeted with them. "Were you serious about taking me dancing sometime?"

Gail nodded. "Yes, I think it would be fun. Were you serious about wanting to go?"

"Yes. I'd like to wear the right shoes, though, like everyone else, so I want to go boot shopping with Susan first." Janet opened her car door.

"Okay. How about you let me know how that goes, and then we can make plans?"

"Okay, I will."

They traded phone numbers.

Janet got into her car and rolled down her window. "Goodnight." She gave a wave of her fingers as she drove off.

Gail returned the wave. She stood there, smiling. She looked forward to taking Janet dancing. It had been too long since she had taken a woman dancing. She danced with women she met when out with Tina and Susan, but it wasn't the same. Janet was just the kind of intelligent, attractive woman she wanted to try again with. She was glad that Janet was even still interested in her since she had really put her foot in her mouth for a moment. Memories of Christine had Gail so out of sorts this evening. It was a wonder that Janet thought Gail had any social skills at all, between the brooding Gail had fallen into throughout the evening and the assumptions she had made about pharmacists and cars. Gail hoped she had convinced Janet that she wasn't a gold digger. Gail wasn't after anyone's money, but she could see how it might have sounded that way. Gail had her own sore points from exes, so she couldn't fault Janet for having hers. Especially since Janet liked her walnuts so much—the woman clearly had good taste.

CHAPTER THREE

It was a gray day in Seattle, and Janet didn't want to be there. On her drive into downtown from the Seattle-Tacoma International Airport, the sky had been gray, the waters of Puget Sound had been gray, the industrial equipment along the waterfront had been gray, and even the trees had seemed gray. Janet attributed her monochromatic view to her bad mood. She had missed out on what had probably been a fun night of dancing last night with Gail and the rest of the women from Tina and Susan's party.

Janet could only imagine what Gail was like on the dance floor. From the glimpses she had of Gail's arms and trim but curvy figure, Janet had a feeling there was a fit, athletic, and alluringly feminine body under all those clothes. And Gail's strong hands...Janet wanted to feel them on her body. The dance floor would be a good place to start.

It would also be a good place to get to know her better. Janet wanted to do that. She was willing to give Gail the benefit of the doubt about what Gail had said about her car, even though the comments had given her pause. Gail probably wasn't a gold digger. No one else Janet had dated since her college girlfriend had been. And Gail had seemed distracted at times during the evening. That was reason enough for an offhand remark to slip out. Janet liked that Gail was sensitive enough to apologize and make the effort to get the evening back on track. She would be sure to follow up with Susan about boot shopping when she got back to Danforth so that she would be ready to go dancing with Gail soon.

Maneuvering a giant sport utility vehicle through the streets of downtown Seattle was not helping Janet's frame of mind about her travels. Many of the streets were narrow, and some were surprisingly steep. The rental car agency that Rockland contracted with had been out of cars in the category that she had reserved and had upgraded her to an SUV. The salesman at the rental car counter had said there would be "no extra charge," as though the inconvenience of not getting the vehicle she had reserved was a treat. The SUV did have a GPS, however, and she had made use of it. It informed her now that she had reached her destination. She pulled the oversized vehicle into the parking structure at Centennial Hospital. She found a parking space, shut off the engine, and sat for a moment to collect herself. It was time to stop these ruminations and get to work. She took a breath, gathered her laptop bag and purse, and got out.

Janet stopped at the front desk to get directions to the Director of Pharmacy's office. Dr. Carolyn Lao greeted her and ushered her into a chair. After some small talk, Janet turned the conversation to the purpose of the visit. "I want to focus on pharmacy preparation for the hospital's upcoming accreditation survey. How do you feel about your department's readiness for the survey?" Most hospitals were regularly assessed by an accreditation organization to verify that certain standards of care were being met in every department. Helping her accounts with survey preparation was a large part of Janet's job, and one that could be tedious in its repetitiveness, as Janet managed multiple pharmacies undergoing surveys in any given year.

"We did well on the last survey, so I hope we'll do well this time too. We've been working hard. Some of the new standards are rather stringent."

"Yes. I brought some paperwork from corporate regarding the new standards. I'd like to go over that information with you after my meeting with administration this afternoon to get an idea of where we're at with those." The organization that conducted the accreditation surveys was always adding new standards, and while some of the new standards would clearly improve the level of care provided, others seemed like busywork and were going to be a hard sell. Janet discussed some more logistics with Carolyn and then asked to see the pharmacy. She planned to look at some specific regulatory and operational areas tomorrow, but she first wanted to meet the staff and get a general feel for this particular pharmacy.

Carolyn led them to the pharmacy and let them in. The usual sounds of a busy hospital pharmacy greeted Janet: labels printing, phones ringing, medication carts rolling, papers being shuffled, packages being opened, multiple voices speaking. As Carolyn described the staffing and various features of the pharmacy and as Janet observed the work, it didn't take Janet long to identify some workflow issues that would need to be addressed before the surveyors came.

Janet caught sight of the wall clock. "Let's go back to your office so I can get my things and head over to my meeting with administration. When I'm done there, I'll come back by your office, and we'll begin going over those new standards."

On Janet's way to administration, her cell phone rang. "Hello?" she answered.

"How are things in sunny Seattle?" her boss Aaron asked.

"Very funny, Aaron," Janet replied with a short laugh. She was still getting used to her new boss and his frequent attempts to be humorous. His joviality didn't always go over well with her when she knew he was sitting in his office and playing computer solitaire while she and his other regional managers were working. Or, at least that was the image that had stuck in her mind after encountering him doing that in his office one day. "I've met Carolyn and some of the others. There are corrections to make before the pharmacy is surveyed, but we'll work on them." They spoke a little more and then said their goodbyes. Janet never understood why Aaron called her on these trips. It wasn't as though he provided any information, other than lame jokes. Janet wondered if Gail had ever had a boss like Aaron. Gail was lucky to get to be her own boss.

Gail stood in the shed at her farm, where she was supervising the packing of produce for Community Supported Agriculture boxes. She was one of the farmers in the area who offered CSA boxes, an arrangement where people paid to receive weekly shares of food from a farm. It was something she believed in. CSA members supported her and other local farmers by paying them directly. In return, the members knew where their food came from and received fresh, seasonal vegetables each week. For the same reason, Gail also participated in the area's weekly farmers' market.

Gail enjoyed interacting with her customers and liked getting feedback from them, so she often stayed to oversee customer pickup of the CSA boxes, and today was such a day. She greeted her customers by name as they arrived, and they smiled and greeted her in return. Many customers lingered after collecting their boxes to chat with her or with each other about which vegetables they were enjoying the most and the types of dishes they had been cooking with them.

When the CSA box pickup was complete, Gail got into her truck. She drove the short distance from the packing shed out to the road and then down the road to her house. Her house was at the end of a long dirt and gravel drive lined by tall oak trees. It was a single-story stone and wood farmhouse situated on an area of land between her walnut orchards and her vegetable row crops. She parked and got out. Bo, her yellow Labrador retriever, ran up to greet her, and she petted him affectionately. He trotted alongside her up the stone walkway to her house.

In the kitchen, Gail looked in the refrigerator for dinner ingredients. Too bad dinner wasn't going to be like last night, when she had eaten with her old friends and Janet. That had been a lot of fun. When she hadn't been thinking of Christine, anyway.

Gail selected a packaged steak to grill, along with some of her own asparagus. There were some leftover mashed potatoes that she could eat tonight too. Gail wondered if Janet liked grilled steak, asparagus, and mashed potatoes.

Gail went outside to light the coals for the barbecue, and Bo followed. She scooped some kibble into his bowl for him. When she came back in, she took the steak out of the refrigerator and seasoned it with salt and pepper. She washed her asparagus, dried it, tossed it with oil, and set it aside. While she waited for the barbecue coals to heat up, she went back outside to toss a tennis ball around for Bo. He was an energetic dog and would bring the ball back no matter how many times she threw it. When the coals were ready, she washed up and got the steak and asparagus. She laid the steak on the grill to cook first, relishing the sizzle.

Janet seemed interested in food. Gail was touched that Janet cared about her contract with the Danforth Bistro and had wanted to help with the situation. At the party, Gail had been surprised to hear herself begin speaking about contracts and sales with Janet. Janet was practically a stranger. She was a good listener, though. Gail rarely discussed her business with anyone except her office manager, Maria.

As Janet had suggested, Gail had provided Susan a list of restaurants for her boss to consider as catering alternatives to the Danforth Bistro. Gail liked the fact that even though Janet seemed to feel strongly about things, she was polite about making her feelings known. Gail had also assigned her sales guy the task of getting a new contract or two to make up for the loss of the contract from the Danforth Bistro.

Gail was careful not to let her thoughts wander too far into the previous evening. She knew that if she got into the memory of Janet's eyes moving over her body as she had carried the platter of food at the party, she may well neglect the barbecue and burn her dinner. As it was, a pleasant warmth suffused her body at the memory of Janet's gaze on her.

Gail flipped the steak and added the asparagus to the grill. She went inside to spoon some of the leftover mashed potatoes onto a plate and microwave it. She carried the plate back outside and added the rest of her dinner to her plate from the grill. She seated herself at her patio table, and Bo lay down by her feet while she ate. Janet had seemed to like the barbecued food at the party. Maybe she'd like Gail's barbecued dinners, as well, if the occasion arose for her to try them.

CHAPTER FOUR

On Saturday, Janet drove over to Susan's house in Sacramento.

"Hi!" Susan greeted Janet with a hug and stepped outside, pulling the front door closed behind her. "Ready to go buy some boots?"

"I sure am. Tina's not here?" Janet asked.

"No, she's working. That's why I thought we'd go today. Tina shares alternating weekends with the other shuttle drivers."

"Are you sure she won't mind the two of us spending time together?" Janet had only just met the couple and did not want Tina to think that anything untoward was going on.

"No," Susan said, giving a quick shake of her head. "She won't mind. It's sweet of you to ask, but she'll be glad that I have something to do while she's at work this weekend. She feels bad that our schedules don't match up when she has to work weekends."

Reassured, Janet offered to drive, but it was decided that Susan would drive since she already knew the way to The Sacramento Western Barn.

Susan navigated them out of the neighborhood and toward a thoroughfare. She glanced over at Janet. "Tell me about your trip. Did you have any of the wonderful fresh fish that I hear Seattle is famous for?"

"Well, I had some salmon, but it was from room service at the hotel. Once it had sat under the dome of the room service tray, it was kind of steamy and wasn't really what I would call wonderful."

Susan made a face. "You didn't go out to eat?"

"No, it's tough to go out to eat on these trips. That's why Rockland tries book us at a hotel with a restaurant or room service. After a day of travel and working on various issues with a lot of different people, usually the last thing I want to do is figure out where to eat in an unfamiliar city and spend time driving to a restaurant when really all I want to do is take a hot shower and relax. It's easier just to eat at the hotel."

"That's too bad. I'm guessing you didn't make it to Pike Place Market or any of the other tourist attractions?"

"No." Janet gave a resigned shrug. "It would have been fun, but there is never really time for much besides work during these visits." Her hotel had been near the Space Needle, and for a moment as she had looked out her window while she ate her dinner at the little desk in her hotel room, Janet had wondered what it would be like to go up to the viewing platform of the Space Needle with Gail and enjoy the view together and maybe go out to a nice meal afterward. But Janet had been there alone, like she always was on a business trip. She glanced at Susan. "You sound familiar with the city. Is it somewhere you want to go?"

"It looks like a fun place to visit. I saw a travel show on it once. It showed the workers at Pike Place Fish Market tossing a giant salmon back and forth."

Janet laughed. "I've seen that on TV too. Maybe you and Tina could vacation there sometime."

"Yes, maybe. I don't think it will be any time soon, though, since Tina just started her job."

"The flight is only a couple of hours if you're able to get a nonstop. You could go for just a weekend if you only wanted to hit the highlights."

"Oh? That's something to keep in mind, then."

Susan and Tina seemed to have a strong relationship. Janet wanted that for herself someday. Maybe she could learn something from Susan. "How long have you and Tina been together?"

"We've been together eleven years and married for one. We exchanged rings years ago, before same-sex marriage was legal." She kept her left hand on the wheel and traced the fingers of her other hand over the smooth surface of her wedding band as she spoke. "We were already committed to each other so we didn't really feel the need to get married, but we did it because we didn't want to miss out on all of the legal benefits." She glanced over at Janet.

Janet nodded. Things like hospital visitation rights and inheritance rights, to name only a couple of the legal benefits, were important and meant so much. They meant that a spouse couldn't be kept from a loved one's deathbed by a closed-minded family, be kept waiting in a hospital corridor, not knowing what was happening, unable to do anything. They meant that children could be provided for, that people didn't have to worry about losing part of their finances.

"You're lucky to have found each other," Janet said.

Susan nodded. "Yes, I feel very lucky." She paused and then gave Janet a sidelong glance. "Would you ever consider getting married?"

"If the right woman came along, yes, I would get married." Janet looked out the window as she considered the idea. She'd never been in a relationship long enough to think that it might lead to marriage. And for so long, same-sex marriage hadn't even been possible. But now it was. The problem was, Janet wasn't even in a relationship at all. If she started dating Gail, would they move in the direction of a relationship? Gail certainly interested her more than any woman in recent memory had.

Janet was pulled from her ponderings by the sight of a fifteen-foot tall boot looming on the horizon. As they neared the boot, a building came into view. Janet turned to Susan with a grin and gestured at the boot-topped building. "I'm guessing that's where we're going?"

Susan grinned back. "Yes, that's where we're going."

"Then it definitely looks like you're bringing me to the right place for boots."

Susan nodded sagely and pulled into the parking lot.

The moment Janet and Susan entered the store, the scent of new leather greeted them. It had to be the boots, but Janet didn't yet see any boots. Instead, what first caught her attention were the displays and racks of women's western clothing on one side of the store. There were blouses, skirts, and dresses like any other clothing store carried, but in distinctive designs that she had never really seen before, except for maybe a few on country-western singers. But many of the clothes were quite attractive.

"We can shop for clothes, too, if you like," Susan said as if reading her mind.

"I see a blouse that I might like try on, but maybe we should start with the boots," Janet said, trying to pull her gaze away from the peach blouse with white floral scrolling that, for some reason, just seemed to call to her.

She followed Susan to the back of the store, and the scent of leather grew stronger. They came to an array of boots against the entire back wall. With such a huge selection, Janet wondered just where she should even begin.

A saleswoman approached. "Do you need any help?"

"We have a lot of looking to do first," Susan said.

"Okay, I'll check back later."

Susan led Janet over to the women's boots. Janet studied the assortment as they walked. There were so many different shapes and styles. And different colors. Even with Trudy talking about turquoise boots at the party, Janet wouldn't have guessed that florescent pink leather boots were an option. "I'm a little overwhelmed by all of the choices."

Susan laughed. "A good place to start is to look at the shape of the toe of the boot. Choose one that you like. Round toed boots or square toed boots are more comfortable for some people, but I think they look kind of clunky."

"Yes, I think of cowboy boots as having pointed toes." Janet strolled along the wall of boots, trying to find a pair that caught her eye.

Susan followed. "I do, too. That's why I have a pair of boots with a snipped toe, which is a pointed toe that is slightly squared off." She paused in front of a pair of boots. "Here's one with a pointed toe."

Janet wondered what kind of boots Gail liked. She looked at the pair that Susan had stopped in front of. "That toe is a little more pointed that what I was thinking of. It looks kind of uncomfortable."

"Yeah. It is awfully pointed." Susan scanned the other choices. "What about that one?"

Janet followed Susan's pointing finger to a pair of elegant brown boots with a moderately pointed toe. They looked like the kind that she imagined a cowgirl might wear. "Yes, that's what I had in mind. I'd like something like that."

"Okay, now let's find a style that you like."

It turned out that most boots came in either distressed or polished leather. The other difference seemed to be the stitched designs on the boots. Some were very ornate while others were more basic. Some boots also had embroidery or inlays. Janet was glad that she had Susan along helping her. Boot shopping was rather involved. Janet felt like she'd been back and forth along the wall a hundred times, but she was determined to find the right pair for herself.

Something finally caught her eye: a pair of distressed brown leather boots with a fancy, stitched shaft. They were gorgeous. She reached out to touch them.

The saleswoman approached. "Find something you like?"

"Maybe. I'd like to try this pair on."

Amazingly, they fit perfectly, and they felt good as Janet walked up and down the aisle to try them out. She paused in front of a mirror. Wearing boots was an experience—they made her feel taller, like wearing heels did, but boots lent her a different air of confidence. She hoped Gail liked her choice of boots as well as she did.

Janet let the saleswoman take her boots up to the register while she continued shopping. She and Susan headed back to the women's clothing section for the embellished blouse that Janet had admired earlier. She held it up. "I hadn't intended to get anything besides boots today, but I do like this blouse."

"You should try it on," Susan said. "It would look great with your blond hair."

"Hmm, I think I will."

"The dressing rooms are just over there," Susan said.

"Okay. I'll be just a minute." The blouse fit. It was more exotic than the blouses she usually wore, but she liked it. Would Gail like it too? Janet paused, staring into the dressing room mirror. Why it did matter so much to her that Gail like her new boots and her new blouse? She shook her head. "Never mind, don't answer that," she said to her reflection. *She* liked the boots and blouse, and she liked exploring this new culture of western wear and line dancing.

They exited the store with Janet's purchases and put them in the trunk of Susan's car. Janet gave Susan's arm a brief squeeze. "Thank you so much for taking me shopping. I really appreciate your help."

"You're welcome. I'm happy to have helped." Susan drove them out of the parking lot.

Janet leaned her head back on the headrest. "I can't wait to go line dancing. Do you think Gail will like my boots? I wonder if she's available to go tomorrow. Oh, but that's such short notice." She stopped herself, knowing that she sounded overeager.

Susan laughed. "I'm sure she wouldn't mind if you call and ask."

But Janet remembered that it was only this past Sunday that Gail, Susan, Tina, and everyone else at the housewarming party had gone dancing together. She sagged a little. "Do you think she will want to go again so soon?"

"I think it will be good for her to go again," Susan said, then grimaced. "I didn't mean for that to slip out."

"Are you talking about how she said she had only been line dancing a few times since leaving Los Angeles?" When Susan didn't respond, Janet guessed again. "Or are you talking about how she gets kind of tense and distant whenever line dancing or Los Angeles comes up?"

Susan shot her a glance. "You noticed that?"

"Yeah. I wondered what it was about."

Susan took another moment to reply. "It's just that those things bring up some memories for her, not all of them pleasant."

"Are you saying that line dancing is unpleasant for her?"

"No, no, I didn't mean that." Susan touched Janet's arm, as though to reassure her. "Gail likes to dance, and I know she wants to take you. I only meant that if she starts going dancing again, maybe she can move past some of the unpleasantness."

Janet was still confused but didn't press Susan on the topic. Maybe she could learn more from Gail herself if Gail brought it up.

After a moment, Susan continued. "Gail has been hurt in the past, and while seeing all of our friends at the party was fun for her, it also brought back memories. I think they will fade, but you might have to be patient."

Janet chewed at her lip. *I can be patient, but I would like to know what I'm up against.*

"I hope that you and Gail will still go dancing?" Susan asked.

Janet nodded. "Yes, I'd like to. I just met her, but I like her." She smiled over at Susan. "You haven't scared me away, don't worry."

"Good. I wouldn't forgive myself if I had."

"Then," Janet grinned, taking her cell phone out of her purse, "you won't mind if I call Gail right now."

"Go right ahead." Susan grinned back.

The call went to Gail's voice mail. Janet left a message saying that she had just bought new boots and asking Gail to call back to make plans.

"Look," Susan said, turning her head to glance behind them while she drove, "we just passed an Italian restaurant that was on the list that Gail gave me for my boss."

"We did?" Janet looked back at the passing storefronts. "Let's turn around. I want to support a place that uses Gail's produce. Let's see what they have."

"Okay." Susan smiled, apparently in favor of Janet's impulsive request. She turned the car around and pulled into the parking lot of the restaurant of Federico's Cucina Italiana.

The menu was posted in the window, and they stopped to read it. House-cured meats, wood-fired pizzas, pasta dishes, salads.

"These pizzas sound really good," Susan said.

"Yeah. 'Wild mushroom, leek, and four cheese pizza.' That sounds like a great combination. It's a little early for dinner, but these descriptions are making me hungry."

"I know. Me too."

"What time does Tina get home? We could get a couple pizzas to go and maybe an appetizer or something to take back to your house and all share. I'd love to treat you for helping me shop today."

Susan smiled. "All we have at home is leftovers, so I think I'll take you up on that. Tina will be home in about an hour. I'm sure she would love some pizza."

"Okay, let's go inside and find out more about which produce of Gail's they use. Maybe that can help us narrow down our choices."

After getting input from a manager, who couldn't say enough about the fresh and lovely produce that the restaurant got from Lawrence Farms and who told her which pizzas and salads best featured the produce today, Janet ordered two pizzas and a large house salad. One pizza was topped with prosciutto, red onion, arugula, and fontina cheese. The other pizza was topped with fennel sausage, thin slices of potato, and mozzarella cheese. The house salad was spinach, carrots, garbanzo beans, and olives with a vinaigrette.

Janet carried the boxes out to the car. "This food smells incredible."

"It does. We better put it in the trunk, or I might not be able to stop from eating some of it on the way back."

"Yes, me neither. Let's lock it away tight," Janet agreed with a laugh.

As Janet drove home after the impromptu dinner with Tina and Susan, her phone rang. When she saw that it was Gail, her heart sped up. She pulled over. "Hi!"

"Hi, I got your message. You sounded excited."

"I am. I had a good time shopping at the western wear store with Susan."

"That's great. I know it's short notice, but would you like to go line dancing tomorrow night?"

"I would love to go tomorrow!" Janet said, unable to contain her glee.

Gail chuckled. "Good, I've been looking forward to taking you."

Janet was relieved to hear Gail say this after what Susan had said. "You don't mind going again so soon?"

"No, I don't mind. Dancing with everyone last week was fun, but I think it would have been more fun with you." The hint of shyness in Gail's voice was endearing.

"That's nice of you to say, especially since I don't know how to line dance yet."

"That reminds me, we need to get there early so you can get the free lessons at the beginning of the evening."

"What time?"

"The doors open at eight, and the lessons are from eight thirty to nine thirty. How about I pick you up at seven thirty?"

"Okay," Janet said and gave directions to her apartment. She hung up, grinning so widely her cheeks hurt.

CHAPTER FIVE

Janet spent a larger portion of Sunday than she cared to admit flitting around her apartment with restless energy. She didn't know why she was so excited about going line dancing. Line dancing had never entered her mind until last weekend at the housewarming party. She'd never wanted to line dance, ever. But now…she did. She told herself that maybe she was just excited in general to be going on a date, since she hadn't been on one since moving out to California from Connecticut. Even so, she hadn't been nearly this excited for any of her previous dates.

When the evening finally arrived, Janet was relieved to be able to start getting ready. She took her new boots out of the box. The boots were just as gorgeous as they'd been in the store, and the new leather smelled wonderful. She ran a hand over the stitching and then set the boots aside to begin getting dressed. She had her new blouse, and she knew she would be wearing snug jeans for Gail, no question, so the only real choice came down to dark or faded. She chose a moderately faded pair to go with her peach and white blouse. She chuckled at the novelty of wearing her boot cut jeans with actual boots. She sat on her bed and pulled on her new boots. She still liked their fit, but the leather was stiff. She knew her feet were going to pay the price for breaking in these boots tonight.

She checked her outfit in the mirror. She was satisfied with the look she had achieved and hoped she would fit in tonight at the bar with the other line dancers. Now for earrings. She chose a pair of gold hoops. She went into the bathroom to apply a touch of makeup, but her hands trembled from her nervous excitement.

"You're being ridiculous," she told her image. "It's just a date. You've been on dates. Just go with the flow." She took a breath and finished applying her makeup.

It wasn't yet seven thirty, so she sat down to flip channels on TV while she waited. When the doorbell rang, her heart leapt and she fumbled with the remote in her eagerness to get to the door. With more calmness than she felt, she smoothed her outfit and went to open the door.

Oh wow, she looks hot! Gail stood tall in an embroidered black long sleeve western shirt with straight leg blue jeans over black boots. Her silver-buckled belt showed off her trim waist and brought out very discreet rhinestone accents in the embroidery across the shoulders of her shirt. Janet collected herself and leaned in to give Gail a hug and say hello. *Mmm, she smells good too.* Gail returned the hug, not too tightly, but enough. When Janet released her, she felt warm and tingly.

Janet cleared her throat. "You look great."

"Thanks," Gail said. Gail's gaze swept over Janet. "You look great too. That's a lovely blouse and a nice pair of boots. Western wear looks good on you."

"Thank you," Janet said with a smile. She felt herself flush from the effect of Gail's eyes sweeping over her, particularly when Gail's gaze lingered ever so briefly at the low-cut waistline of her jeans. And Gail's compliment alleviated any fears she had about fitting in tonight at The Pink Stallion.

Gail shifted her feet. "Are you ready to go?"

"Yes," Janet said. She stepped out, locked the door, and started down the stairs. She knew that her jeans hugged her hips and thighs, and wanted to give Gail a nice, long look.

At the bottom of the stairs, Janet turned and looked back. "So if it's not a car, is it a truck or is it a motorcycle?"

Gail's eyes moved up to Janet's face.

Janet quirked a smile, happy that Gail's attention had been focused where she had wanted it to be.

Gail gave Janet a sheepish grin and relaxed her grip on the stair railing. "No, it's not a motorcycle. It's that white truck, there. I use a truck for my farm." She pointed to a new-looking Ford F150.

A truck. Janet should have guessed that a truck would be a more practical vehicle for Gail. They walked over to the truck. Gail unlocked and opened the passenger door for Janet then rounded the vehicle and got in. The seats in the truck sat much higher than those in Janet's car. It felt kind of nice.

"It still has that new car smell," Janet said. "New truck smell, I mean."

Gail chuckled and started the engine. "I bought it just recently. It's a good thing too, because I wouldn't have wanted to use the old one to take you out. It's too worn from farm use."

"I'm sure I could have managed, but this one is nice," Janet said.

"Yeah, I like it." Gail headed in the direction of the nearest freeway on-ramp to Sacramento.

Janet made conversation, telling Gail about her boot shopping experience with Susan. She also mentioned discovering the Italian restaurant with the great pizza that was a testament to the tastiness of Gail's produce. Gail seemed to like that; she kept smiling as Janet talked, and asked about Janet's workweek. When Gail described her own workweek and her CSA program, Janet mentioned that she had belonged to one in Connecticut. "It was only available in the spring and summer, though."

"Because of the weather?" Gail asked.

"Yes."

"We don't have that problem here. I'm glad I don't have to battle snow and frozen soil." She smiled. "You seem interested in food. Any particular inspiration?"

Janet shifted in her seat. "Well, my grandparents were farmers, dairy farmers. Whenever I visited them, my grandma was always cooking something. She used to trade some of her dairy products for eggs or fruits and vegetables from her neighbors, who were also farmers. I loved the taste of her food."

"It sounds like you were close."

"Yeah, I miss her." Janet was appalled to feel her eyes suddenly mist over with tears at a sudden memory of her grandma's loving smile. She missed her grandma so much sometimes. But she couldn't believe she was about to cry on a first date. She opened her purse for a tissue and dabbed at her eyes.

Gail glanced over at her with concern. She extended her hand across the center console toward Janet.

Janet accepted her hand and held it between her own. "I'm so embarrassed. I'm not sure what brought that on. My grandma passed some time ago. I didn't mean to get emotional." She let out a shaky breath.

"It's okay, don't be embarrassed."

Janet sniffled. "I think I'm okay now." She gave Gail's hand a grateful squeeze before releasing it. "I would sign up for a CSA here, but it's too tough with my schedule. The pick-up days are either when I am out of town or just before I leave town again."

"You could try the farmers' market," Gail suggested.

"I like to go to the farmers' market but my schedule only sometimes allows me to do that, so I usually just go to the grocery store. The produce in the stores here is fresher than that where I used to live."

"Yes, we're lucky to have such nice growing conditions here in California." Gail glanced over again at Janet, as though checking that she really was okay. "How about the radio?" Gail reached to tune it to a pop station. "Is this okay?"

"Sure, I listen to this station too." The upbeat music was helping take her mind off her grandparents. "Huh, I just thought of something. Do they only play country music on line dancing night? I don't really know any country music."

"No, they play a mix. You don't have to know any of the songs, anyway. Just listen to the beat."

"Okay, good. I can do that." Janet wondered if she could ask another question about line dancing without causing Gail to tense up like she had at the party. She cleared her throat. "So, um, how did you get into line dancing?"

Gail's hands tightened a little on the wheel, her knuckles whitening against the black vinyl. Then, slowly, the tension went out of them. "Well," she said, "remember how I mentioned that Tina, Susan, and I all worked in downtown Los Angeles? We all used to hang out sometimes after work. There was a club in the area that we all went to one night. It happened to be line dancing night, and we all had a good time trying it. It became a regular thing for the three of us to go." She paused. "And for our other friends to go."

"You mentioned that you had only been line dancing a few times since moving back to Danforth. Why did you stop going as often?"

Gail's hands were flexing on the steering wheel again, and Janet wasn't sure if she was going to answer. "It wasn't the same. I just got out of the habit." Gail took a deep breath, abruptly relaxed her grip, and changed to steering casually with one hand. She cleared her throat. "Maybe I'll have a reason to start going line dancing again if you like line dancing."

"Maybe you will," Janet agreed coyly.

"Here we are—The Pink Stallion." Gail pulled into a parking lot next to a large brick building that could be considered nondescript but for its sign involving a neon pink outline of a horse rearing up on its hind legs, the neon flashing so that horse seemed to be in motion.

Gail turned to Janet. "There's no coat check, so you might want to leave your purse here. You can just slide it under the seat or put it in the console, but bring your ID."

"I doubt they're going to card me. I'm forty-one."

"They check everyone's ID at the door. I'm forty-two, and they card me."

"Oh, okay." Janet hadn't been carded in years. She took her driver's license out of her wallet and began getting some cash also.

Gail reached over to still her hand. "No need, this is my treat."

Gail's fingers were warm, comfortable against her hand. When Gail withdrew them, Janet missed the sensation on her skin. Janet put away her wallet and slid her purse under the seat.

As Gail had said, a bouncer checked their IDs at the entrance. Gail paid both their cover charges, and they walked in.

Pop music was playing, and Janet took in the spacious dance floor in the center of the room. There were colorful strings of lights along the rafters and large round light fixtures that gave off a warm glow. Janet liked the high ceiling. She had been in some bars with such low ceilings that the rooms became a little claustrophobic as the night went on. One wall was taken up with a long bar, and there was a group of small tables set off to the side along another wall. The only western decor to speak of were the cowboy hats the bartenders were wearing and the country music videos playing on a TV. When Janet remembered that line dancing only took place one night per week, the eclectic decor made more sense.

Janet turned when she felt Gail's hand on her shoulder. "Would you like to have something to drink while we wait for the lessons to start?" Gail raised her voice over the music.

Janet nodded. "Sure, a drink sounds good. How about a whiskey sour?"

"Whiskey sour coming up." Gail headed for the bar.

Janet surveyed the other patrons. It was early, but people were arriving in a steady stream. Tina was right—it was a nice, mixed crowd. Not only were there a lot of women, there were various ages and ethnicities. Most women were wearing jeans. A lot of the women were wearing tight, long sleeve knit shirts with decorative fronts and V-necks, but Janet saw everything from sweaters in deference to the cool Sacramento night to tank tops despite the temperate weather. She saw western-style blouses like hers and Gail's, and she saw a lot of big western belt buckles on men and women both, plus the occasional cowboy hat. Most everyone was wearing cowboy boots, but some wore sneakers or flat dress shoes. However, one woman was wearing high-heeled sandals and another was wearing high-heeled fashion boots. Janet had no idea how they were going to dance in that footwear and wondered if they were beginners like she was.

Gail returned with drinks. "Why don't we sit at one of the tables? I got us some snack mix too."

Janet accepted her drink with a "thank you" and followed Gail to a table. Gail had gotten a whiskey sour for herself as well. Janet took some of the pretzel and nut mix that Gail set between them.

"What do you think of the place?" Gail asked.

"I like it. It seems like a good crowd."

Gail nodded and sipped her drink.

Janet tapped her fingers to the beat of the music. "Are you going to join me when they start the lessons?"

"I can if you want me to."

"Yes, join me. I'll feel better if I don't leave you sitting here to watch me make a fool of myself while I try to learn the steps."

"Okay, but I don't think you'll make a fool of yourself. There are always a lot of beginners. Just have fun with it."

Janet admired Gail's confidence. Janet wished she could be more like that and worry less tonight—not that Janet was worrying so much as just feeling a little self-conscious in this new environment with more experienced dancers around her. She and Gail continued to sip their drinks and eat the snack mix while they waited and watched more people file into the bar.

The music stopped, and a woman with a hands-free, around-the-ear microphone walked out to the dance floor. "Hi, everybody, and welcome to The Pink Stallion! We're glad you're here with us to line dance tonight. I'm Cassie, and I'm going to give some lessons this first hour for all you beginners. We'll start out with some basic steps, and then we'll do a beginner dance or two. For those of you who already know how to line dance, feel free to join in if you want to get warmed up. Sound good?"

The crowd responded with enthusiastic cheers and clapping. There were even a few whoops of excitement. Janet grinned.

"Okay, everybody who wants to learn to dance, come on out here!" The music resumed. Cassie waited while people gathered. Janet and Gail got up from their seats and walked out to the dance floor with the others.

"Let's get warmed up." Cassie began clapping and stepping from side to side. Gail and the other dancers did the same, and Janet followed suit.

"Okay, now let's get started. I'm going to teach you something called the Grapevine. We call it the Vine for short. It's in a lot of the dances, so we'll get it down first." She turned around so that she was facing the same direction as everyone else. She stood with her feet slightly apart, pointed to her right, and said, "We'll do it to the right first." She instructed the group while she demonstrated the steps. She stepped her right foot right, crossed her left foot behind her right foot, stepped her right foot right once more, and then scuffed her left foot next to her right. She demonstrated the scuff by kicking her foot forward while scraping the heel. "Everybody with me?"

The steps were simple enough, but the movements were new. Janet hoped Gail wasn't watching her too closely yet. She glanced over and was relieved to see that Gail wasn't scrutinizing her moves at all but rather just moving easily with the steps.

"Now, Vine to the left." Cassie repeated her instruction and demonstration of the steps, but to the left. "Let's do both sides again."

Janet was glad for the repeat. In her new boots, it was tricky getting the hang of stepping her feet behind one another, but she was glad she had boots for the scuffing part. She looked to the side again to admire Gail's steps. Gail smiled and nodded encouragingly at her. Janet smiled back. Cassie took the group through it a third time.

"Let's add some more steps," Cassie said. "We're going to walk backward and tap, then we're going to do step taps and end with a scuff." Cassie demonstrated. Janet was getting the hang of it; at least, she thought she was. She certainly seemed to be doing just as well as the other beginners around her. Cassie took them through the sequence of steps twice again.

"Let's put it all together now, starting with a Vine to the right." Janet, Gail, and the others followed Cassie as she did the couple steps to the right then a scuff, the steps to the left then a scuff, the steps back, the steps back and forth, and the final turn and scuff. Because of the turn, everyone was facing the next wall. Cassie took them through the dance a few more times until they were facing the wall they had started from. "Congratulations, everybody! You've just done the Electric Slide! Give yourselves a hand!" Janet and the others assembled clapped and smiled happily.

"We have time to learn another. Do you want to?" Cassie cupped her hand around her ear and cocked her head at the group.

The group cheered and clapped. "Okay, then, let's learn Slappin' Leather," Cassie said.

Janet turned to Gail excitedly. "That's the one from the party!"

Gail grinned. "Yeah, it's a fun one to do. This might be a little different, though. The girls did a short version at the party."

Gail was right. Cassie started the dance out with some of the moves they had just learned for the Electric Slide, and Janet didn't remember that from the party. Cassie demonstrated some other new moves, as well. Janet appreciated that Gail had mentioned the difference so that she could watch for these subtleties about line dancing as she was learning.

Cassie arrived at the point of lifting and slapping boots. Balancing in boots to bring the foot back and out and forward to slap was harder than it looked, and there was a bit of stumbling among the group. Boots added another dimension to the dancing, though, and Janet was glad she had bought them. Some of the other dancers had had to slap sneakers instead of slap leather.

Cassie led them through the steps a few more times. The steps were manageable enough when Cassie took them through it slowly, but at tempo Janet's feet missed a few. She missed fewer steps as Cassie repeated the moves. At least she had managed not to get her feet tangled up like some of the others had.

Cassie finished. "Give yourselves another hand!" The group applauded, and Cassie curtsied. "Have fun out here tonight!"

Janet discreetly wiped her brow. She turned to Gail, who was looking a little flushed herself. "Do you mind if we take a break?"

Gail's breath caught at Janet's beauty as Janet turned to face her after the dance. Janet's blue eyes were bright, and her cheeks were flushed a healthy pink. Her rising and falling chest from the exertions of the dance tightened the fabric of her pretty peach-colored blouse across her breasts. Had Janet just asked a question?

"Gail?" Janet asked. "Just a quick break? Maybe we could sit for a moment?"

"Oh, sure, yeah," Gail said. Gail was certain that she must be flushed herself, if not from the dancing, then from the movement of Janet's breasts as her chest rose and fell. She felt her nipples tighten. This was going to be tough with the evening just starting. She ran a hand through her hair and took a breath. "Are you thirsty? Can I get you another drink?"

"Yes, but how about a club soda this time? I want to be able to learn the steps without tripping myself." Janet smiled.

"Good idea. I'll have one too. How about grabbing us a table, and I'll be right back?"

Janet nodded, and Gail headed for the bar. Gail could get used to dates like this. It was so refreshing to be on a date with a woman who was just being herself and not trying to play weird mind games. In Gail's experience, women seemed to think that a good game plan was to at first try to appear disinterested or unaffected. Gail appreciated that Janet was open with her feelings and didn't feign nonchalance about things. Janet was clearly excited to be here dancing, and Gail was looking forward to dancing with her more.

The bar was crowded now and the bartenders busy. Gail got the attention of one and placed her order. She paid and picked up the two glasses of club soda, each of which had a lime wedge on the rim and a little straw. Gail looked to the tables for Janet. Now that the beginner lessons were over, the regulars were arriving, and the room and dance floor were filling. But Gail had no trouble locating Janet in the crowded room. Her lovely blond hair and radiant beauty stood out.

Gail wove her way through the crowd to Janet's table. She placed a glass of club soda before Janet and sat down with her own.

Janet gave her a smile. She took the little lime wedge off the side of the glass and squeezed a few drops of lime juice into her drink before taking a sip. "Oh, this is refreshing. Thank you."

"My pleasure." Gail took a drink of her own club soda. The cool, bubbly liquid did feel refreshing.

Janet reached over, clasping each of Gail's hands in either of hers and smiled again. "And thank you so much for bringing me here tonight. I'm having a lot of fun."

"I can tell. I'm really glad you're enjoying it."

Janet gave her hands a nice little squeeze before releasing them. She sat back, and a little frown marred her forehead. "I'm concerned that this might all be a little boring for you since you're not a beginner."

"No, not at all. I'm having fun too. I love your enthusiasm for things. It's fun to be here with you." Gail touched Janet's arm. "Besides, you're picking up the moves, and I'm looking forward to dancing with you later." She smiled.

"So it's not all group dances?"

"No, there are partner dances too."

"Cassie didn't teach us any of those." Janet bit her lip.

"I can teach you. We can do a simple one when the right music comes on."

"Okay. I'd like that." Janet finished her drink.

Gail finished her drink as well. "In the meantime, are you ready to try some more line dancing?"

"Yes." Janet nodded emphatically.

Gail stood up and extended her hand to Janet, who reached for Gail's hand and stood. Gail tucked Janet's hand through the crook of her arm and led her to the dance floor.

Janet liked Gail's gentle but take-charge manner and appreciated her clearing a path through the crowd. A few groups of line dancers had formed on the dance floor. Gail explained that since the DJ had not announced any particular dance, free dancing was allowed. Gail led her to a group doing a dance involving some of what Janet now recognized were the basic moves. Gail found a space to join in, guiding Janet to a space alongside her. Gail started moving through the steps like a seasoned pro, and Janet did her best to emulate her and to remember Cassie's instructions.

Since this line dance, like many of the others, it seemed, began again every time the dancers ended up facing another wall, there was an opportunity for Janet to practice each time around for a total of at least three repeats of the steps. Even so, this was a lot different than learning when Cassie slowly instructed everyone, and Janet was missing some steps. It was going to take a lot of practice get all the steps and dance smoothly like Gail.

The DJ began playing a new song and announced a dance called "Honky Tonk Stomp." Gail leaned close to Janet and said over the noise, "If this is the beginner version of this dance, it will be a good one to try."

"Okay."

"Let's find a spot." Gail took her hand and began guiding her to a space in the middle of the dance floor. Janet hesitated. She really didn't want to be in the thick of things before she knew what she was doing.

Gail must have sensed her hesitation. "It's tempting to stay in the back or to the side when you're a beginner, but with all the turns, you might end up in the front. The safest place is actually in the middle."

Janet was once again grateful for Gail's tips on the subtleties of line dancing. She was relieved when the dance started with heel fans then heel digs and taps like she had learned in Slappin' Leather. In doing steps that she had already learned well, she wasn't missing things like she had moments ago. At one point in the dance, everyone hitched one leg and turned before doing another Vine sequence and stomp. Gail and some of the other dancers had their thumbs hooked in their belt loops or hooked in the waist of their pants during all of this. Gail's casual manner impressed Janet, especially during the more intricate steps. Janet kept her own hands free to help with her balance. The dance began again facing another wall, and Janet was able to relax a little as the steps repeated. Dancing the same steps in sync with everyone in a group was tough, but it was fun too.

The song ended, and another began. Gail turned to Janet as the DJ announced the dance. "This one is kind of complicated, so why don't we sit it out?"

Janet shook her head. "No, I'll sit it out. You should dance it. You must be tired of beginner dances."

Gail hesitated, and Janet could tell that she was torn between not wanting Janet to sit on the sidelines while she danced and really wanting to dance. Janet placed a hand on her arm reassuringly. "Go ahead, I don't mind. I'll be fine." Janet moved off the dance floor and stood at the perimeter to watch.

Everyone on the dance floor started stepping. It was easy to keep sight of Gail. She was tall and even taller in her boots, and her well-cut figure, flattered by her western wear, stood out in the crowd.

Janet loved the sight of all the women dancing together. Hips moving, legs working. It was a little hypnotic. She liked watching Gail most of all. Apparently, so did a woman in the row behind Gail. The woman's eyes were practically glued to Gail's ass. Janet was surprised that the woman hadn't tripped or bumped into adjacent dancers yet.

"Hi, sugar." A woman's voice said. "You new here?"

When no one replied, Janet realized that the woman had been talking to her. Janet turned to find a woman with a somewhat weathered but not unattractive face and with long hair pulled back in a ponytail. The woman was looking her over like Janet was a tasty piece of meat.

"I'm here with someone," Janet said and looked away.

"Well, whoever it is left you all alone. We should get to know each other."

"Thanks, but I'm not interested." Janet moved away.

Gail turned on her heel to face another wall and repeat the dance steps with the other dancers. She was facing Janet's direction now and easily spotted her in the crowd as before. But Janet wasn't alone now. There was a woman standing with her, leaning close to talk to her, looking as if she was about to stroke Janet's arm.

Gail wanted to kick herself. *What was I thinking leaving a date as attractive as Janet alone in this bar full of women? Of course she's going to be hit on. I should go over there and do something about it.*

Gail was surprised at herself. She'd never had this reaction to someone flirting with a date. And she couldn't just storm off the dance floor to confront the woman with the ponytail. Janet would think she was crazy. For all she knew, Janet might already think she was crazy after all of Gail's distress over just trying to answer Janet's simple questions on the drive over. It was just that the questions made her think of Christine, and Gail hadn't wanted to think about her ex on the first date, let alone talk about her.

Gail kept her eyes on the ponytailed woman. Gail didn't know Janet well enough to know her views on dating, but Gail dated only one woman at a time. Not that that had mattered to Christine. Gail was relieved that Janet didn't seem to be paying the ponytailed woman much attention. Good, Janet wasn't interested. Janet moved away from the woman, and Gail felt even more relieved. But that didn't stop the constriction in Gail's chest or the turmoil in her mind.

Trying to put distance between herself and the ponytailed woman, Janet stepped around people until she found another good vantage point from which to watch Gail dance. Janet wondered how long it would take her to be able to dance as well as Gail. She wanted to be able to participate in more of the dances, like the one going on right now. Maybe there were lessons that she could take somewhere in Danforth. Line dancing would be a fun way to liven up her exercise routine, and if she learned more, she could come here again with Gail and do these trickier steps. But if lessons were available, would they fit into her schedule?

The dance ended, and the DJ switched to a slower song. Couples moved onto the dance floor. Janet saw Gail scanning the crowd for her and moved so that Gail could see her. Janet liked how Gail's face brightened when Gail caught a glimpse of her. Gail began striding to her in that purposeful manner of hers, and the way Gail gazed at her gave Janet a little shiver of delight.

Gail stopped before her. "We can do a partner dance to this song, if you would like to give it a try."

"Yes, I'd love to give the dance a try." Janet extended her hand to Gail, and Gail took it in her own.

"Just follow my lead, and you'll do fine." Gail led Janet to a space on the dance floor and drew her into her arms. "Put your other hand on my shoulder. Okay, this dance is very simple. It's called the Country Two-Step. We're just going to do two steps quick and then two steps slow."

Janet felt the gentle side-to-side and forward leaning from Gail and instinctively knew where Gail meant for her to step and with which foot. Which was good, because it was hard to concentrate with Gail's warm right hand on her torso and the inside of Gail's forearm nearly brushing her breast. Janet managed to keep dancing, taking another step backward and then two more. Gail repeated the quick-quick-slow-slow pattern. The movement of Gail's firm shoulder muscles beneath Janet's hand only added to the distraction. Janet was beginning to think she'd end the dance by stepping on Gail's foot and then pitching into the other couples.

"Would you like to try a turn?" Gail asked with a smile.

"Okay." Janet smiled back.

"I'm going to turn you to the outside." Janet turned into the light pressure that Gail applied with the hand on Janet's torso and twirled with the guidance of Gail's other hand. When the turn was complete, Janet continued with the two-step as seamlessly as she could.

"Very nice!" Gail said.

"Thanks." Janet grinned. "You made it easy."

"You made it easy too. You're a good partner."

The DJ changed to a song with a faster beat.

"Would you like to dance more, or are you ready to leave?" Gail asked.

Although Janet was still having a great time, her feet were feeling the effects of dancing in her new boots. "I'm ready to leave if you are."

Gail led them out of the bar and into the cool night air. "God, this air feels good," Gail said.

"Doesn't it?" Janet exclaimed. She was tired but exhilarated. Even though she had only had one cocktail, she felt somehow buzzed. She was excited and alive after this new experience, and it was all because of Gail. She rarely went out and had a good time like this anymore. She twirled around in front of Gail like she had just done inside during the Country Two-Step. "Whew! Tonight was so much fun!"

Gail laughed.

Janet came back into step alongside Gail. "Thanks again for bringing me."

"You're welcome. It was my pleasure." She put her arm around Janet as they walked to the truck. Janet leaned into her embrace.

On the drive back to Danforth, Gail chatted with Janet about some of the dances. It had been too loud in the bar to say much and was easier to talk now. As they continued the drive, Janet looked like she was winding down. Learning all those dance steps was fatiguing, Gail knew. And Janet's muscles would probably be sore tomorrow.

Gail glanced over and felt a smile tug at her lips at the sight of Janet trying to stifle a yawn. The yawn escaped her, and Gail chuckled. Janet looked over with a sheepish smile, and Gail gave her a smile back.

Gail parked in a spot on the street in front of Janet's apartment. She got out of the truck and rounded it to open the door for Janet.

Janet gathered up her purse and seemed to get out gingerly. "Something tells me I'm going to be sore tomorrow," Janet said.

Gail opened her mouth to offer an apology, but Janet spoke again, "No, don't worry. It was well worth it." Janet stepped closer and linked her arm through Gail's. A delicious warmth spread through Gail's limbs at her touch.

They walked arm-in-arm to the staircase leading to Janet's apartment. When they reached the base of the stairs, Janet unhooked her arm from Gail's and turned to face her. Janet's gaze dipped to Gail's mouth. Janet's lips were slightly parted and looked oh-so soft. Janet stepped closer and then leaned across the remaining space to place a gentle kiss on Gail's lips.

A wave of desire swept through Gail the moment Janet's lips touched hers. After dancing alongside her all night, and holding her in her arms, it was hard to show restraint, but somehow she managed it.

After the kiss, Janet stood back smiling, only to again drop her gaze to Gail's mouth. A thrill ran through Gail when Janet leaned in to kiss her again. This kiss turned harder, and Gail responded in kind.

She settled her hands on Janet's waist to keep them from wandering. She willed them not to drop to Janet's buttocks that were encased by those ass-hugging jeans, and willed them *especially* not to give those buttocks a squeeze or use them to pull Janet's hips closer to her. Gail broke the kiss, breathing a little heavily now. "I, um…" She cleared her throat. "I liked your goodnight kiss."

Janet smiled. "I liked yours too." She fell silent.

Gail wanted to say something, to ask if she could come in, or wanted Janet to invite her in, but she knew it would probably be a mistake this first date. She didn't want to push things this evening, and something told her that Janet probably didn't invite a woman up to her apartment on the first date. "It's late. I'd better go."

Janet licked her lips and nodded.

"Good night." Gail headed back to her truck. She turned to watch Janet go up the stairs to her apartment.

Gail stood waiting next to her truck to see that Janet got into her apartment safely. When Janet unlocked the door and turned to wave at Gail, Gail waved back. Then the door closed and Gail went home, alone but happy.

CHAPTER SIX

Monday morning, Janet woke up sore and stiff from dancing in her new boots. She stretched her body out slowly and made no move to get out of bed just yet. Dancing worked different muscles than the elliptical trainer did. She lay there, staring at the ceiling, feeling twinges in muscles she didn't know could have twinges. Was Gail sore too? Maybe she was, since she said she didn't go dancing much anymore. Janet couldn't imagine why Gail had stopped going dancing, given that she obviously enjoyed it. And Janet couldn't imagine having as much fun dancing with anyone else. Or sharing such a wonderful goodnight kiss with anyone else. Janet wanted more of those kisses and had been sorely tempted to invite Gail up to her apartment, something she didn't normally do on a first date.

Janet wiggled her toes and rotated her feet at the ankles. It was not going to be pleasant to put on pumps tomorrow for work. She had to fly to Tucson to visit another hospital pharmacy. It felt too soon to leave town again, but at least she didn't have to leave today. That was the only reason she had been able to go dancing last night.

Her flight departed at six a.m. tomorrow, which meant she needed to be at the airport at five, which meant she needed to leave the apartment just after four, which meant she had to get up at...well, way too early.

She knew she should get out of bed. She needed to check the Rockland website, pack her luggage, and get prepared for tomorrow's trip. She let out a sigh, at which a random abdominal muscle gave a throb of protest. But she had to get up. There was no sense putting off the inevitable. She got out of bed and slipped out of her bedclothes to take a hot shower, looking forward to having the heat of the water help soothe her sore muscles.

Gail winced slightly as she swung her leg to straddle her all-terrain vehicle to drive out into her walnut orchards. Her sore muscles were a reminder that she was out of practice at line dancing. Poor Janet. She must be feeling the effects of the night of dancing even more than Gail was.

But Janet was right—it had been worth it. Gail had enjoyed herself so much last night. In fact, she had felt happier than she had in a long time. Janet was wonderful company, a good dancer, and...a good kisser. Gail was glad that her own moronic comments about Janet's car hadn't prevented the date from happening. Janet seemed to have set any gold-digging concerns aside.

Gail wished she could do the same with her own worries. All the dancing of this past week had resurrected memories of Christine. She wished that Christine hadn't made her so mistrustful. She'd been so cautious of relationships ever since, the better not to get hurt. She'd avoided getting too attached to anyone, avoided any connections that might endanger her heart. But so far it hadn't been very hard, because she hadn't connected enough with any of the women she had dated for things to progress to a relationship.

She felt something with Janet, though, that was for sure. The very thought of her sent her pulse racing. Even so, it was going to be hard to put herself out there with her. Opening herself up and spending more time with Janet would increase the potential of ending up with a wounded heart yet again. Gail wasn't sure if she would be able to take that risk.

Gail guided the ATV along the dirt border of the first orchard on her property. Even though she had her orchard manager Patrick, she liked to inspect the orchards herself every so often. Now that it was May, and the orchards were in their second month of irrigation, she needed to check the irrigation lines, make sure everything was getting watered, and that there were no leaks.

Cruising on to the next section of orchard, she noticed a dry patch. She guided her ATV in for a closer look. Yes, this area was definitely getting less water. She dismounted from the ATV to inspect the micro sprinklers and the lines, but they looked intact. Maybe there was a clog or maybe the water discharge rate needed to be adjusted. Now she would need to check the water flow meter, which was more work than she had expected this morning. Patrick should have noticed the dry patch and taken care of the problem. This was the very reason she had to come out here and check things herself. Could she trust no one?

She got back on the ATV and drove to the small flow meter at the head of the irrigation line. She stared down at it. It was damaged. Had it been broken by the equipment used during the recent mowing of the orchard row middles? She would ask Patrick to follow up. In the meantime, she would go buy a replacement small flow meter and take care of the problem herself.

After finishing with the other sections of orchards and finding no further problems, Gail headed the vehicle to her house. Bo ran out to her as she approached and then ran alongside the ATV as she drove in. Putting the ATV into park, she reached to ruffle Bo's fur along his shoulders. "Hey, boy. How are you doing?"

He wagged his tail and panted, turning to lick her hand, which Gail took to mean he was doing fine.

Gail stepped off the ATV. "I've got to go buy a part, but I'll be back soon."

Gail drove her truck into town to the agricultural hardware store. She saw that Pam, her old high school friend, was working the register today. Pam was busy scanning a customer's purchases, so Gail just waved and headed back to the aisle for irrigation supplies. Finding what she wanted, she came to the register.

"Hi, haven't seen you in a while," Pam said.

"Well, nothing has broken in a while," Gail kidded. She set her small flow meter on the counter. "How have you been?"

"Good. I'm seeing a new man, and things are going well."

"Good for you," Gail said. Pam had complained about her last boyfriend being lazy.

Pam rang up her purchase. "How about you? Are you seeing anyone?"

Gail hesitated.

Pam's round face broke into a smile, as it so often had when they had played soccer together on their high school team. "You are! You are seeing someone!"

Gail's face heated. Her relationship with Janet was so new and special that she wasn't sure she wanted to share details just yet. She lowered her head to busy herself getting cash out of her wallet for the purchase.

"Ooh, is she pretty? Is it serious?" asked Pam.

Pam was one of the only people Gail had come out to back in high school, and she'd taken a proprietary interest in Gail's love life ever since. "Relax, Pam," Gail said with a chuckle. "I've only been on one date with her. And yes, she's pretty." Gail handed Pam the cash.

"I can't remember the last time I saw you blush, so I'd say it was a good date."

Gail nodded. She was still smiling and, much to her chagrin, still blushing.

Pam handed Gail her change and put her purchase in a bag.

There were other people in line now, so Gail didn't linger. "We should get together soon and finish catching up."

"Definitely. Call me." Pam started ringing up the next customer.

Outside in her truck, Gail took out her cell phone. She just wanted to hear Janet's voice and say hello.

"Hi, Gail!" Janet answered. Gail could hear the smile in her voice, and instantly felt a smile spread on her own face.

"Hi," Gail said. "So, I'll confess. I was a little sore today. Were you?"

"I wasn't going to admit it, but yeah."

"Not too bad, I hope?"

"No, not too bad anymore. I feel pretty good after I soaked in the tub today."

The mental image of Janet's nude body made Gail's mouth go dry and her pulse kick up. She struggled for something to say as her mind continued to fill with images.

"Now I'm packing," Janet said.

Packing? She didn't mean…packing, as in dildos, did she? No, that didn't make sense. Janet hadn't been packing last night. Gail supposed it could be interesting, but…

"Do you like light blue or yellow better?" Janet asked.

"Uhhh…" Maybe Janet really was talking about dildos. But where did she find such assorted colors? And wasn't it a little soon in their relationship to be talking about this? Gail would be open to dildos, but fingers suited her just fine. Her groin pulsed at the thought of being inside Janet, with or without a dildo.

"Come on, help me decide. I really don't know which color sweater set I want to take to Tucson for work tomorrow because I like them both," Janet said.

Ohhhhh…*that* kind of packing. Gail shook her head at herself and a laugh escaped her lips. *I really need to get it together, or Janet's going to think I'm un-dateable.* She took a breath. "I'm sure either the blue one or the yellow one would look good on you."

"How did I know that's what you would say?" Janet said with feigned exasperation. "Well, I think I'll go with the light blue one."

"It'll look great on you."

"Thanks. I love sweater sets. They hardly take up any room in my suitcase, and they rarely wrinkle. I still need to choose a business suit, but don't worry," Janet said, teasing, "I won't ask what color."

Gail chuckled.

"What have you been doing today?" Janet asked.

Gail described her day inspecting irrigation equipment in the orchard and shopping for a replacement for a broken part.

"I'd love to see your farm sometime," Janet said.

"I'd love to have you over."

"Great! But…I hope I didn't seem like I was inviting myself."

"No, that's okay. I'll be glad to show you. The orchards are pretty right now. Would you like a grand tour when you get back into town?"

"Yes, I think I would."

"What day do you get back?"

"Thursday. So, I could come to your farm on Friday."

"Okay, that's fine for me. We can talk later in the week to figure out the details."

After the call, Gail shook her head at herself, tapping her phone against her forehead. What was Janet going to think of her now that a simple conversation about packing had thrown Gail from her game? It was just that when Janet had started the phone conversation by mentioning soaking in the tub, the mental image of Janet's nude body had made Gail's mind go to sex. It was not much of a leap for someone who had hardly slept a wink after that arousing goodnight kiss to think of dildos at the mention of packing. Gail sighed. Thank God she'd kept it together.

* * *

Janet collapsed onto the couch in her living room. It had been an exhausting three days in Tucson. She'd spent most of the days *and nights* analyzing documents from the pharmacy and the hospital billing department. What Aaron had thought would be a simple matter of correcting some charge capture problems had turned out to be more involved. It probably should have been a three-night stay, but Aaron and his secretary hadn't arranged it. Janet had even had to use her layover in

Phoenix to finish up some of the work. At least she got some sleep on the flight back to Sacramento and so hadn't sounded totally exhausted when she called Gail back to arrange the farm visit for tomorrow at one o'clock. That visit to see Gail was something she had looked forward to all week.

Janet took her laptop out of its carrying case and plugged it in at her desk. She had made up her mind to take line dancing lessons, so it was time for some research. She should also probably call Susan and tell her how the new boots had worked out.

"Hello?" Tina's voice answered the call.

"Hi, Tina. This is Janet. How are you?"

"Hey, Janet! I'm doing well. How are you?"

"A little tired, but just fine. The boots Susan helped me pick out worked great for my line dancing date with Gail. We had a wonderful time. I feel like you made it all possible by inviting me to your housewarming party."

"That's great, but don't give me too much credit, or it might go to my head."

Janet heard Susan's voice in the background. She heard sounds of the mouthpiece being covered and Tina's muffled voice say to Susan, "It's Janet." There was an excited squeal, more muffled conversation, and then Tina came back on the line with a chuckle. "I think I better hand the phone over to Susan. She has lots of questions. I know she'll fill me in later. Talk to you soon!"

Susan came on the line. "Tina said you had a great time—tell me all about it!"

"We did have a great time. Line dancing with Gail was a lot of fun." Janet recapped some of the evening's experiences. "I was really glad to have the boots. I think I would have felt out of place otherwise."

"I'm glad they worked out."

"They did, and I'm going to get a lot more mileage out of them, because I'm going to sign up for line dancing lessons."

"You are?"

"Mm-hmm. I want to get better at it. Gail was sweet enough to do the lessons at the start of the evening with me and all of the beginner dances, but I don't want her to be bored if we go again."

"I don't think she would be bored. And I doubt that you need to bother with lessons. None of us have had lessons. You'll pick it up."

"I probably would, but I guess I'd like to pick it up faster to catch up to everyone. Besides, it will be something new for my exercise routine. After I get some practice, maybe we can all go dancing sometime."

"That would be fun! So, you're seeing Gail again?"

"Yes, I'm going out to her farm for a visit tomorrow."

"That's wonderful!"

"Yeah, I can't wait to see her again after we had such a good time dancing." And kissing, but Janet kept that to herself.

"You be sure and call us with a dancing invitation any time."

"Okay, I will." Janet hoped things would continue to go well. She wanted more dates and more dancing with Gail.

CHAPTER SEVEN

Janet turned off the road and onto the drive that she hoped led to Gail's farm office. The gravel drive was lined on either side by tall, overhanging trees, and she glimpsed leafy green row crops on the other side of the trees. Gail had said the farm office was just past a packing shed at the end of the drive. Janet hadn't really thought of farms as having offices, but she supposed they must, just like any other business. She pulled past what must be the packing shed—a big, square building with oversize rolling doors—and parked her car beyond it. She took a deep breath to steady her nerves.

Janet got out of her car, balancing a tray of cookies and her purse as she shut the door. This morning, she had done some baking. After practically inviting herself over, she didn't want to show up at Gail's doorstep empty-handed. Janet figured that cookies were usually welcome. Everyone liked cookies, right?

Gail came out of the office, and Janet felt a rush of heat. God, but Gail was beautiful with those dark eyes and those strong cheekbones. She was wearing a forest-green T-shirt, relaxed jeans, and work boots, and managed to look fit, attractive, and comfortable all at once.

"Hello!" Gail called cheerfully.

Janet returned her greeting and gave Gail a quick hug and a kiss on the cheek. She handed her the tray of cookies. "Here, I made these this morning for you and your staff. They're walnut bar cookies. I hope you like them."

Gail brought her hand to her heart and smiled, obviously touched. "You baked me cookies? Thank you so much."

"You're welcome," Janet said.

"Let's take them inside, and I'll introduce you to Maria." Gail held open the door for Janet and followed her inside.

A professionally dressed older woman came out from where she had been seated behind a wooden desk. "Janet, this is Maria Montez, the office manager," Gail said. "Maria, I'd like you to meet Janet Webber."

Janet shook the woman's hand and gave her a smile. "Pleased to meet you."

Maria gave her a cheerful smile in return. "And you."

"Janet brought some homemade cookies for us." Gail set the tray down.

Maria looked with interest at the tray of cookies. "Oh, I love cookies with filling. I know these won't be good for my figure, but I can't resist homemade cookies." Maria eagerly unwrapped the tray and offered it to Gail and Janet, who each took a cookie, and then she took one herself.

Gail sighed in contentment as she chewed, and her eyes closed for a moment. "These are delicious."

"They are," Maria agreed.

Janet was pleased that her cookies were a hit. "I'm glad you both like them."

"They're just as tasty as they look," Maria said.

"Yes, I love the walnut filling," Gail said.

Maria waved her almost-eaten cookie around. "Gail mentioned that you're a pharmacist, but you could trick me into thinking that you're a baker."

Janet grinned. "I can't take all the credit. It was my grandma's recipe."

Maria turned to Gail. "I bet our customers would love these."

"All these sugary walnuts between two layers of buttery cookie…who wouldn't love them?" Gail said, reaching for another.

Janet contemplated the cookie in her own hand. "Have you ever considered selling a product with your walnuts?"

"You mean like cookies?" Gail asked.

"Or just anything with walnuts. Even something simple, like candied walnuts or spiced walnuts. If the Danforth Bistro is any indication, it seems like people who buy your walnuts see them as interchangeable with other walnuts. If you made a product, you would have something unique that people would only be able to get from your farm."

Gail nodded. "A value-added product, I believe it's called. That's an interesting idea for us." She looked at Maria, who was smiling.

"Yes," Janet said. "If the product was popular, it would probably make your plain walnuts more popular too."

"Let's look into it," Gail said to Maria.

Maria nodded. "Yes, I can even do that now. The idea has gotten me curious too." She moved back to her desk and computer, ostensibly to get started.

Gail finished the last of her cookie. "Are you ready to see the rest of the farm?"

Gail led Janet out to her truck. "The walnut orchards are down the road, and the row crops are somewhat spread out, so the best thing is probably to drive."

As Janet climbed into the truck, she glanced back at Gail. "I hope I wasn't interfering back there."

"Interfering?" Gail asked. "Do you mean the idea about a walnut product?"

Janet nodded. "I didn't mean to make work for your office manager."

"No, you weren't interfering. I'm always glad to hear a business idea, especially from someone as interested in food as you are. And I can tell that Maria is just as interested in your idea as I am."

"The idea popped into my head, and I thought that maybe I had overstepped by mentioning it."

"No, don't worry about it. Maria will check into it and tell me if it's feasible. If it's something that could work here, that's great. If not, that's okay, too."

Janet nodded and seemed to relax.

Gail drove down the dirt road out to where the row crops started. She rolled her window down and rested her arm on the sill, letting the smell of the countryside drift over her. She described to Janet what was growing now in May, indicating the fields as she spoke, until she slowed the truck. "Here's a good place to stop. We can check on my zucchini."

Gail stepped out into the field. Janet followed more carefully, easing her way out of the truck and onto the dirt road and then onto the looser soil in the field. The sight of Janet in the afternoon sunlight captivated Gail. Her blond hair shone, and her skin had taken on a healthy glow in the warm weather. She looked so beautiful that it made Gail ache.

Gail gestured at the zucchini growing on the vines. "This group is the first of the season and should be just about ready."

Janet smiled and came to stand beside her. "I love zucchini this size, before they get too big. They're so tender. I go to the farmers' market just for that."

"Yes, these are very popular with my CSA customers too. Would you like some to take home with you?"

"Sure, if it's all right," Janet said.

"All right?" Gail injected a teasing tone into her voice. "I hear that I'm the boss of this place, so of course it's all right." She was gladdened when Janet laughed, a gentle, ringing laugh that went right through her. Gail walked over to her truck to get a folding knife with which to cut the zucchini from the vines. She knelt, selected several of the small zucchini that Janet had said she liked, then straightened and handed them to Janet, cautioning her to avoid the small prickles on the stems.

"Thank you." Janet arranged them gently in her hands.

"You're welcome." Gail loved that Janet admired the vegetables as if they might be a bouquet of roses. Gail gave her a grin.

They got back into the truck, and Gail drove Janet in the direction of the walnut orchards.

Janet leaned forward and peered through the windshield as they approached the rows of the big, leafy walnut trees in the distance. The sun was shining on the trees, bringing out the deep green color of the large, almost glossy leaves.

As Gail drove closer, she pointed out to Janet the little balls of light green that were the young walnuts in their hulls hidden among the leaves.

Gail stopped the truck to give Janet a closer look at the trees and the young walnuts. She and Janet got out and walked into the first row of trees in the orchard. Janet gazed up at the dense canopy of leaves. The sun did not penetrate to the orchard floor, and a refreshing coolness pervaded the area. Gail smiled as Janet let out a satisfied breath after inhaling the fresh, earthy scent of the orchard.

Gail gestured to a grouping of green walnuts hanging from a branch. "In the fall, the hulls will split open to reveal the walnuts, and we'll be ready for harvest."

Janet turned to Gail, as though about to ask a question, but caught her foot and stumbled.

Quickly, Gail reached out and wrapped her arms around Janet, supporting her.

Janet clutched Gail for balance. As Janet regained her footing, Gail loosened her tight hold. Janet loosened her grip also but did not remove her hands from Gail's shoulders. "Are you okay?" Gail asked.

Janet was looking at her lips the way she had that night after dancing, and Gail's pulse kicked up. Janet searched Gail's eyes and leaned closer, obviously more than just okay. Gail pressed her lips to Janet's and kissed her slowly, enjoying the feel of Janet's soft lips against her own again. Desire overtook Gail, and she intensified the kiss, tightening her arms around Janet's shoulders and reveling in the sensation of Janet's body against hers.

Janet gave a little hum of pleasure.

The sound made Gail realize herself. She slowly broke the kiss and loosened her arms from around Janet's shoulders.

Janet stared longingly at Gail's lips, her eyes hazy with desire and her lips still parted. It was almost enough to make Gail wrap her arms around her again and pull her in for another kiss, but she was too turned on as it was, and the orchard was no place for more. Instead, Gail made a show of studying the area on the ground where Janet had stumbled. There was a portion of exposed tree root. She poked at it with the toe of her boot. "This must be what tripped you," she said. "I'm sorry."

"It's not your fault. I was looking at the trees instead of watching where I was going." Janet straightened her clothing and brushed a stray strand of hair out of her face. "Besides, you caught me. Nicely, I might add." She smiled.

Gail smiled back and then ducked her head modestly. "Maybe we should go to the house now." *Oh, why did I say that? Great, she probably thinks I'm trying to haul her off to my bed now.* "I mean...we can relax there. At the house. We can sit down, I mean. Outside. On the patio." She rubbed the back of her neck with a hand. "Maybe have some iced tea." She took a deep, calming breath and let it out.

"Iced tea would be nice," Janet said nonchalantly.

In the truck, Janet glanced at Gail. She still looked a little flustered after inviting her back to the house. Janet had considered teasing her but couldn't do it. Gail was too sincere and too gentle to tease.

As they approached a lovely stone and wood farmhouse from a back drive, Janet started at the sight of a big yellow dog who came bounding and barking excitedly across the backyard.

"There's no need to worry," Gail said. "That's just Bo. He's a big baby."

Janet looked more closely at the dog. He looked like a Labrador. She tended to like Labradors because they always looked like they were smiling. She tried to relax.

When they reached the house, Gail parked the truck and turned to Janet. "Wait here a moment so I can get Bo before he jumps all over you."

Once Gail was holding the dog firmly by the collar, Janet got out of the truck. The dog was happily wagging his tail so much that his entire body was moving.

"Bo, I want you to meet someone. This is Janet."

"Hi, Bo." Janet extended a hand for him to sniff.

Bo gave her hand a brief sniff then licked it twice with his lolling tongue.

"Bo!" Gail said.

"It's okay. I'm glad he likes me." Janet petted his head while he continued to wag his tail and pant.

"Let's go inside, and you can wash your hands while I get us that iced tea." When Bo tried to follow them, Gail shut the door. "You stay here, Bo. We'll be back out soon."

Janet washed her hands at the kitchen sink. The window above the sink overlooked the walnut orchards, giving a great view of the leafy green trees. She dried her hands and leaned back against the counter to take in Gail's kitchen. The ceiling was slanted high with exposed wooden beams. There was another sink at a granite-topped island that was large enough to fit four stools along the other side. The island was in the middle of a polished hardwood floor. "This makes me miss my house in Connecticut. It kind of reminds me of my own kitchen. Not that my kitchen is as nice as this, but cooking in my apartment here in Danforth is not the same."

Gail looked up from filling two glasses with ice cubes, a frown on her face. "You still have a house in Connecticut?"

"Yeah. But I'm trying to sell it. I wonder if my realtor is making any progress. I should give him a call."

Gail poured tea from the refrigerator into the glasses. She handed one to Janet. "Why don't we sit outside?"

Gail pulled out a chair at the patio table for Janet and then sat down in another one. Bo came over to Janet, and she petted him. Janet sipped her tea and looked up at the tall tree that provided shade to the table and to most of the backyard.

"It's an oak tree," Gail said.

"It's so pleasant out here. This was a good idea." Janet watched as Bo went over to Gail for more pets. Janet sipped her tea. "I want to apologize for the other night."

"The other night?"

"For thinking that you were a gold digger. It's obvious that you're not."

Gail shook her head. "No, no, it's I who should apologize again for saying those ridiculous things."

"I shouldn't have jumped to conclusions."

"No, really, it's okay. I can't say that I blame you after what I said."

Janet was glad that the conversation wasn't going to be a sore point between them. She took another sip of her tea. "It seemed like we covered a lot of distance in the truck today. How big is this farm?"

"One hundred and ten acres. There are seventy acres of walnut trees, and forty acres for the row crops, including my house."

"That's a lot of land."

Gail shrugged. "Yeah, but there are so many costs associated with farming that the profit margins are fairly small. No one's getting rich by growing vegetables. It's something of a labor of love for a lot of us. The walnuts bring in more money."

Janet had the feeling that Gail was being modest. Gail obviously did fine for herself, and Janet was glad to know that money had, in fact, been a non-issue in their date.

"How long have you been farming?"

"Since I moved back here six years ago." Gail paused. "It's funny how things work out. I never imagined that I would be back here. The last thing I wanted to do when I grew up was farm like my parents. But I missed it." She swept an arm out at the orchards. "I missed this environment. When my parents retired, I decided to buy their house and farm. It turned out to be a good decision. I love it here."

"It shows. I can tell that you enjoy your work." Gail had looked relaxed and happy on the farm today, clearly a woman in her element. "What did you do before this?"

"I was a financial analyst at an investment bank," Gail said with decidedly less enthusiasm.

"That was your job in Los Angeles?"

"Yes. I had a desk job in a high-rise." Gail chuckled mirthlessly and shook her head. "It was what I thought I wanted, to get as far away from farming as possible. I was good at my job in Los Angeles, and the money was good, but the job just wasn't me."

"I know what you mean," Janet said faintly. "Your parents must be glad that the farm is still in the family so that they can come visit."

"Oh, they don't visit. They're not really comfortable with my being a lesbian. They visited me once in a while in Los Angeles but didn't like seeing me with women and stopped visiting altogether when I moved in with my girlfriend. But, I guess they liked southern California better than they let on, since they live there now."

"I'm sorry," Janet said. "My parents are like that too."

Gail shrugged, as if to say, "What can you do?"

Janet shifted a little in her chair. "Tell me about this girlfriend you lived with."

Gail's lips twisted. "I didn't mean to bring her up. She's not worth talking about."

Janet sensed that this might be the source of Gail's anguish about Los Angeles. "She hurt you, didn't she?"

Gail gave a slight nod as she ran an agitated hand through her hair. She shifted in her chair, leaning forward and resting her elbows on her knees, staring at a distant point, apparently lost in memories.

When no answer from Gail was forthcoming, Janet tried to lighten the mood. "Was she as bad as my gold digger?"

Gail snorted. "Only if your gold digger liked to have quickies with strangers in bathroom stalls while you were both out line dancing with your friends."

"Oh…" Janet let out in dismay. Janet could only imagine how hurt and upset she would feel if that happened to her. No wonder Gail seemed so unsettled when it came to line dancing and Los Angeles. Janet would be reluctant to relive such an experience by going line dancing again either.

Abruptly, Gail stood up and went to get a ball that was at the edge of the patio. Bo got up and wagged his tail expectantly. Gail threw the ball forcefully, and he ran after it. "Her name is Christine," Gail said. "We were together five years. She told me that what happened at the club was just a one-time thing and meant nothing." She raised her shoulders in a helpless shrug. "If it was nothing, why do it?"

"Yeah," Janet murmured. Five years. That must have really hurt. And for Gail's partner to be so casual about it? What a slap in the face.

"I was faithful to Christine. I guess I took it for granted that she would be monogamous also." Bo brought the ball back, and Gail threw it again.

"No, don't say that." Janet got up and walked over to Gail, placing a hand on her arm. "That's not an unreasonable expectation to have."

"Well, she thought it was," Gail said bitterly. "It would have interfered with the fun she was having with the woman I found her with."

"What ended up happening?"

"I wanted Christine to move out, but she kept making excuses about how she couldn't find an apartment." Gail grunted and shook her head. "I ended up moving out instead." Gail again threw the ball for Bo.

This Christine was something else, not taking responsibility for the pain she caused. Janet wouldn't forgive her for making the otherwise confident Gail feel so vulnerable. It was beyond Janet how anyone could cheat on a woman who seemed to be the whole package as Gail did. Janet reached for Gail, putting her arms around her in a comforting hug. "I'm sorry she hurt you." She felt some of the tension leave Gail's body as Gail relaxed into her embrace.

After a long moment, Gail pulled back from Janet and let out a breath. "Thanks. I'm okay now, I think." She took her seat at the patio table.

Janet returned to her seat as well and sipped her remaining tea. She appreciated that Gail had opened up to her. She decided to do the same in return. "I envy you for having found a career that you enjoy. I can't say as I've ever been as enthusiastic about mine as you seem to be about yours."

"No?" Gail asked, sitting up straighter, her expression opening at leaving the topic of Christine.

"No, and on top of that, my job and my work schedule has always been such a recipe for a girlfriend breaking up with me."

Gail tilted her head. "How so?"

Janet paused. She hoped that Gail's returning good cheer would last once Gail saw where this topic of conversation would eventually bring them. She'd start slowly and ease Gail into it.

"Earlier in my career, when I was a staff pharmacist in a hospital, I had a long shift and a long commute each way, making for long days. And nights, on the occasions that I had to work the evening shift. I couldn't stay out very late on dates or even go out some evenings at all with that schedule."

Gail nodded. "At peak times on the farm, the days can really stretch, so I know all too well what you mean."

"Add weekends and holidays into the scheduling mix, and I was really unavailable."

"That kind of schedule would be tough."

Janet nodded. "Then I was a Director of Pharmacy for a while."

"Was that any better?"

"Not really. Maybe my schedule was a little better, but the job wasn't. I really didn't like being involved in hospital politics and playing the games that have to be played with administration and other departments. And it was difficult to leave it all at the office at the end of the day. Plus, I had to carry a hospital pager so that I could be reached at any random time if for some reason the pharmacy staff couldn't handle problems in my absence. Dates don't work very well when a pager goes off in the middle of them."

"No, probably not."

"In my current job, I travel most weeks. What date wants to put up with that?" Janet realized that she'd done nothing but prove she was impossible to date. She wondered if Gail was ready to run in the other direction yet.

"Well," Gail said slowly, "I would think that if someone were dating you, she would understand that travel is part of your job."

"Maybe, but so far that hasn't been my experience." Janet took a breath, preparing herself to point out that her business travel might be a big problem, given Gail's history with Christine. "Not only does no one really want her girlfriend flying out of town and unavailable, but also no one really wants to wonder about her girlfriend staying in hotels on the road all the time."

Gail suddenly looked like a deer in the headlights.

Janet sighed. "See what I mean about my job?"

Janet knew that Gail wasn't naïve and would have eventually realized the possible implications of her constant travel without the need to have them pointed out, but Janet had wanted to hasten the process before she and Gail became too involved. It would be too hurtful to become attached, only to have Gail realize that she didn't want a girlfriend who was on the road all the time. "I can only imagine what's going through your mind, given how your ex hurt you," Janet said. "I'm sure a girlfriend who is a business traveler would be a big worry for you."

Gail gnawed at her lip a little. "I recently made an agreement with myself that I should stop worrying that relationships are going to end badly before I even let them get started." She looked at Janet. "We're only just getting to know each other, so I'm going to take my own advice and not start worrying already."

Janet studied her. Janet had become pretty discouraged when it came to dating and to relationships, but maybe it was time she approached things with a new outlook like Gail seemed to be doing. Gail's resolve impressed her. "I think that's good advice for me too." She reached for Gail's hand and smiled. "I enjoy spending time with you, and if you're not going to worry, I'm not going to worry either."

Gail smiled back, and their eyes held. "I enjoy spending time with you too." She reached to place her free hand lightly behind Janet's neck, gently guided her closer, and kissed her.

Janet savored the tenderness behind the kiss. It had been a long time since anyone had kissed her like that.

Gail drove Janet back to the farm office where she'd left her car. After giving Janet a kiss goodbye, Gail went into the farm office to see if any cookies were left. At first, she thought the staff must have eaten them all, but she laughed in delight when she saw that Maria had set aside a couple for her.

Gail sat down in the empty office to enjoy the cookies. She thought about Janet and how easy it was to talk to her and how much she liked being with her. How much she liked kissing her. Gail rarely brought a date home, but it was different with Janet. Was a tour of the farm a date? Gail wasn't sure, but it had seemed like one. Just as it had seemed natural to invite her to her house. Gail thought about how wonderful it felt to catch Janet in her arms in the orchard and how it had felt even more wonderful to kiss her again. Gail's chest became pleasantly tight and warm.

It had been startling, though, to hear that Janet still had a house in Connecticut. Gail was relieved to hear that Janet was trying to sell the house. But was there anything else in Connecticut that Janet missed? Connecticut was all the way across the country, and Gail didn't like to think that Janet might be drawn back there for something. Or worse, for someone. Even though they had just met, the thought of Janet moving back was awful. It was bad enough that Janet had to fly away from Danforth each week, but at least she came back each time.

Even more startling was the revelation about the opportunity that Janet would have each week to easily cheat on a girlfriend if she wanted to. Gail felt foolish for not considering Janet's job from that angle sooner. Thoughts of Christine crept back. Janet wasn't like Christine, though. She wouldn't have pointed out those possible implications of her business travel if she were like Christine, would she? She had offered reassurances that it wasn't unreasonable to think that girlfriends should be monogamous, hadn't she? Gail shook her head at herself. She clearly wasn't out of the worrying habit yet.

CHAPTER EIGHT

Even though Long Beach was in state, travel there had taken longer than either of Janet's trips to Seattle or Tucson. Rockland company policy was to choose from among the lower-priced flights even if the flights were longer and involved multiple stops. Janet hadn't been able to book a nonstop flight this time because there had been too much difference in price, and her flight had involved a layover at Los Angeles International Airport. What could have been travel of about an hour and a half had taken three times that. She was trying not to think about how she would face the same thing on the way home.

Janet envied Gail's wonderfully short commute each day. She imagined that farming was a lot of work, but it was hard not to romanticize being outside in the daylight and fresh air, growing things. All those trees, all those plants…it was soothing. No wonder Gail had left Los Angeles to return to the family farm in Danforth.

The Long Beach hotel Janet was staying in belonged to one of the nicer hotel chains that Rockland contracted with. It featured a gym, and after a long day grappling with problems in the pharmacy, Janet intended to burn off some of the stress with a good sweat.

She'd expected to find the gym deserted as she often did in a hotel, so she was surprised to find that there were other guests there. She could see why they were there; it was a nice gym. It was spacious and had a full array of equipment and machines. A woman was power walking on a treadmill and another was riding a recumbent bicycle. Both nodded a greeting to Janet and then returned to watching the TV on the wall while they exercised.

Janet was pleased to see an elliptical trainer. It was a different brand than the one at her gym in Danforth, but she found the buttons to select a program similar to her routine. She pumped the pedals and handlebars, getting her legs and arms warmed up. She breathed deeply, feeling the tension in her body begin to release. She glanced occasionally at the TV on the wall, but her brain was too busy rehashing the stresses of the workday to pay much attention to what was on. The machine increased the resistance, and Janet stepped harder to keep up. Her legs and buns were starting to burn. A middle-aged man came in and headed to the weight machines. He was probably going to do a circuit.

The programmed machine changed to less resistance, and the burn in Janet's muscles reduced to a more tolerable level. Janet sensed eyes on her. She glanced around. The middle-aged guy was using the lat pulldown machine now. Janet was pretty sure that the stare she had felt was his, since he was not making any effort to look away now. She looked away and continued exercising. She hoped he didn't come over. She wanted to work out, not be stared at or hit on. A few minutes later, she felt a presence alongside her. The man was now standing nearby.

"Hi, I'm Rick. I thought you could use this." He extended a towel to her.

The women on the treadmill and recumbent bicycle turned. They eyed Rick, rolled their eyes at each other, and then resumed their exercise.

"No, thank you," Janet said. She had seen the basket of towels at the side of the room only after she had gotten on the machine and started her workout. While she wouldn't mind having a towel on which to dry her hands that were now a bit too sweaty from her workout to comfortably hold the moving handlebars of the elliptical trainer, she wasn't about to accept anything from Rick.

He continued to hold the towel out to her. "Are you sure? You look like you could use it."

Wow, tell me twice that I look so sweaty that I need a towel. Smooth pickup game you've got there. "No, thank you," Janet repeated.

Apparently getting the message that Janet wasn't interested, Rick returned to the weight machines. Good.

The elliptical trainer kicked into a high level, but Janet was now annoyed enough at Rick's intrusion that she didn't even notice the burn in her muscles. Only when she began breathing heavily from the exertion, did she realize that she was working hard. Janet got hit on enough at some of the hospitals she visited, and she didn't need to get hit on in the hotels too. It was like she had told Gail: there were plenty of opportunities for cheating. People were away from their spouses and thought they could have a fling. Did Rick not think that Janet hadn't seen his wedding ring? Just because they were in a hotel together, Rick thought they could start something? So presumptuous and so annoying. And just so thoughtless to his wife. Janet reached the cooldown of the program, and slowed her steps.

Returning to her hotel room, Janet called room service to place an order for dinner and then took a shower. By the time she had toweled off and dressed, room service arrived with her meal.

A delicious aroma wafted through the steam vent in the domed lid, and Janet eagerly lifted the lid. Mmm, the grilled chicken breast and rice pilaf looked good. But the side of humongous and very thickly crinkle cut slices of zucchini accompanying them—not so much. Janet knew that the oversized zucchini would be tough and strong-tasting. It was nothing like the fresh baby zucchini that Gail had given her.

Janet had cooked those on the weekend before leaving town. They were so fresh that all she did was slice them, fry them in olive oil in a skillet and season them with salt and pepper. She had eaten them with a pork chop and a salad, and they had been delicious. Janet pressed at one of the huge zucchini slices with her fork, but it would not break in half. She ate the chicken and rice.

As she ate, her mind drifted to her visit to Gail's farm. Janet thought of their kiss in the orchard and the feeling of Gail's strong arms wrapped around her. It had been all she could do to keep her hands off Gail when they got to the house. She was glad she and Gail had talked instead, though. Janet appreciated hearing about the ex-girlfriend in Los Angeles. She was glad to know what bothered Gail so much about LA.

It had been good to get more of her own relationship difficulties out in the open, as well. At the last part of their visit, when Gail had driven her back to her car at the farm office, Janet had mentioned that she had signed up for a beginner line dance class. Gail hadn't hesitated to say that she would take her dancing again. There was potential for something with Gail, and Janet knew Gail felt it too. Now at least they were aware of each other's histories.

Janet poked at last of the rice. She missed Gail already, strangely enough. It would be a while until they could see each other again, but maybe Janet could call while waiting here in Long Beach. She got out her phone and pressed Gail's number.

"I just had dinner and wished that I had some of your vegetables instead of the vegetables they served me," Janet said when Gail picked up.

"Your food was bad?" Gail asked. "I'll be glad to give you more vegetables when you get back."

"That sounds great. I'll tell you that I could have eaten a lot of them tonight. I was hungry from busting my butt in the hotel gym."

"Oh? I can tell you that whatever butt-busting you do at the gym pays off, because your butt certainly looks spectacular in jeans."

Janet broke into a smile. "Thanks. I'll be sure and wear a pair the next time I see you. Between my workday and getting hit on by some annoying guy, I had a lot of energy to expend on the elliptical trainer."

"What? Somebody hit on you?"

Janet immediately realized her mistake. She hadn't meant to remind Gail of the relationship pitfalls of business travel. "Yeah, some guy in the gym. I sent him away."

Gail was quiet on the other end of the phone.

Janet feared that Gail was getting caught up with worry, which would be ridiculous for Gail to do, given Rick's persona. At least the person hitting on her hadn't been one of the other women in the gym, because that would no doubt worry Gail all the more. Janet silently chided herself for letting the pickup attempt slip out. She could just imagine Gail's mind filling with ideas of hookups in the hotel gym.

Janet heard a woman's voice in the background over the sound of the TV. "Is someone with you?" Janet asked.

"Yeah. My friend Pam is here. We're watching a women's soccer exhibition game on TV and having a pizza."

Janet was quiet. She wanted to know if Pam was just a friend but didn't want to ask. It hadn't crossed Janet's mind that Gail would be anything other than monogamous in a relationship. Not that they were necessarily at a stage where Janet should worry about such things, but the thought of Gail with another woman gave her an unpleasant feeling in the pit of her stomach.

"Pam and I played on the soccer team together in high school and have been friends ever since. She's straight."

"Oh," Janet said. "I didn't mean to—"

"No, it's okay. I would wonder the same thing if I were you."

Janet didn't argue about her own transparency. It wouldn't have fooled Gail, who knew plenty about worry and suspicion. Janet was just grateful that she wouldn't have to spend a restless night or several wondering who the other woman was.

"I'm not interested in dating anyone else while I'm dating you," Gail said.

Janet's heart thudded so hard she thought it would burst. "That's nice to hear. I feel the same." She hoped Gail understood that she was no Christine.

CHAPTER NINE

Thursday evening, Janet pulled on her cowboy boots. Even though she was tired from the repeat of the long layover on her trip home from Long Beach, she was looking forward to her first formal line dancing lesson.

She arrived at the dance studio a little early. As she approached, she caught bits of conversation from her potential classmates.

"My therapist said I should try a new activity," said a woman with permed, frizzy hair. The very overweight man she was talking to wiped his brow with a handkerchief. He was sweating profusely even though the dancing had not begun. "Yeah, my doctor said I should exercise. I have cowboy boots, so I thought why not try this?"

Janet was relieved to hear that he had his doctor's okay to exercise; he certainly didn't look healthy. She hoped that the pair was also here to have some fun like herself, and that everyone wasn't just taking this class out of medical necessity. Janet glanced at two other potential classmates, a middle-aged man and woman waiting quietly on a bench. She took the opportunity to introduce herself and learned that they enjoyed ballroom dancing but wanted to branch out into other kinds of dance.

It was nearly time for class to start. Just as Janet was wondering if the class would be only the five of them, a group of three women of retirement age walked in, alongside a woman who looked to be in her early twenties. One of the older women was telling the young woman that she and her friends thought that learning dance steps would be just as good for the brain as doing crossword puzzles and would be more fun, too, since it was something they could all do together. The young woman nodded and smiled and then stepped to the front of the room.

"Hello, everyone," she said with a bright smile. "This is beginning line dancing. I'm Natalie Forrester, and I'll be your instructor." Natalie was fresh-faced and fit, with long brown hair pulled back in a loose ponytail. She wore faded jeans, a button-down, short-sleeved shirt, and worn boots. As Natalie described her background—she was a college student studying veterinary medicine—Janet was amused by how she paced energetically in front of the group, like she just couldn't wait to get started.

"While there are many line dances, they all have common steps," Natalie said. "Even the advanced dances have steps in common with the beginner dances. The trick is to master different step sequences and then be able to put them together to do the dances." She picked up a remote and pointed it at the sound system, pushing buttons as she spoke. "This first class, I want to teach you a dance called Flying Eights. It's a fast, fun dance and consists of some of the steps I'm talking about. First, I'm going to demonstrate it so that you have an idea of what you'll be learning tonight." Country music started, and Natalie set down the remote and then demonstrated the dance.

The dance started with a Vine to the left. At the end of the Vine, Natalie hitched one leg and clapped. Then she did a Vine to the right, ending with a quarter turn to do a Vine to the left toward another wall. At the end of that one, she did a spin, then did a few marching steps toward them, and then did a few steps where she hitched each knee high while stepping and clapping. There was a smoothness and fluidity to her steps.

Natalie stopped the music. "That was Flying Eights!" The class applauded, and Natalie gave a quick bow. "Okay, let's break down the sequences. But first, I want you to arrange yourselves into two rows of four."

They started with the Vine, then went through the other parts of the dance, step by step. Natalie had everyone practice multiple times until each segment was learned. Janet appreciated her pace and patience. Compared to the quick lesson at The Pink Stallion where Janet had sometimes felt like she was sinking rather than swimming because the steps had only been repeated enough for people to get the general feel of them, this pace was leisurely. With the repetition, the steps and the form were becoming ingrained, and Janet knew that she and the rest of the class were going to be able to get the moves down well with Natalie's instruction. By the end of the class, they were all dancing the Flying Eights, albeit to differing degrees. Janet liked the feeling of mastering the dance.

After class, Natalie approached Janet. "You look like you've done this before."

Janet smiled. "I guess you could say I had a trial by fire at The Pink Stallion a couple of weeks ago. They cram a lot into the lesson at the beginning of the evening. And then, I practiced all night on the dance floor with my date helping me."

Natalie nodded. "Ah, that explains it." She tapped a finger to her chin thoughtfully. "You know, I think that you're kind of in between the class levels. I think you might find this beginner class a little slow going, but I think the next class level might be too much until you've mastered more steps. Private lessons might be helpful, if you're interested."

"Hmm," Janet said. She did feel more advanced than this beginner class, and she knew that it was from already having done a variety of dances the other night. "Are you the instructor?"

"Yes, and the lessons would be here also. The owner lets me use the studio. We could start next week and do them right after I finish this class, if you like."

"That sounds great!"

When Janet got back to her apartment, she drew herself a bath. The short lesson hadn't been as strenuous as her night of breaking in her new boots with Gail at The Pink Stallion, but she hoped to minimize any soreness with a nice soak. She sat back and extended each foot in turn under the tap as the tub filled. As the hot water covered her body, she reached forward to turn off the faucet and then reclined with a sigh of pleasure.

Her thoughts returned to the evening's dance lesson. It had felt good to dance again, and she looked forward to her private lesson next week. Private lessons weren't something she would have thought of, had Natalie not suggested it. She was impressed that Natalie found time to give lessons during what must be challenging studies. Janet would be glad to learn at a pace specifically geared to her; what was more, the extra money for the private lessons would be going to a college student who she was sure could use it.

Janet finished her bath and then reached to flip the lever to drain the tub. Nothing happened. She jiggled the lever but still the tub did not drain. *Great.* She stood up, grabbed a towel, and got out. She regarded the still full tub with dismay. Would it still be full tomorrow, or would the water at least slowly leak down the drain so that she would be able to shower the next day? She made a mental note to submit a maintenance request to her landlord as soon as the apartment building office opened in the morning.

Her phone rang from her bedroom, and she ran in to grab it. "Gail...hello." Janet realized too late that her annoyance at her malfunctioning bathtub showed in her voice.

"Is this a bad time?" Gail asked.

"No, not at all. I've just been fighting with my bathtub."

"That's a new one. Did you win?"

Janet laughed. "I'm not sure yet. I'm still breaking in my boots so I thought I would soak my legs and feet in the tub, but then the lever to drain the tub wouldn't work so the tub is still full of water." Janet gave a frustrated sigh.

Gail made a sympathetic sound. "It sounds like the bathtub trip lever linkage may need to be adjusted or replaced."

Janet wasn't sure what that was. "I plan on filling out a maintenance request form first thing tomorrow, but I already know what my landlord is going to say. He'll say that for a non-emergency it will be at least a week before the plumber can come by. I had to wait that long before when water was dripping from the toilet tank. I told him that water was dripping on the floor, but he said just put a bucket under the tank. I was changing out the bucket for a week before the plumber came and replaced that little metal tube running from the tank to the wall to take care of the problem."

"The toilet connector," Gail said. "I can fix the bathtub drain for you, if you like."

"You know how to do that?"

"Sure. I've fixed a lot of things on the farm and at the house over the years."

Though Janet appreciated Gail's offer of help, she knew that plumbing repairs could be complicated and expensive. "I should probably wait. That way, my landlord will cover the cost of the repair since it's included in my rent."

"The part probably only costs ten dollars or so. I can come fix it tomorrow after work, if you like."

Janet reconsidered. Gail made the repair sound simple. Janet would love not to have a malfunctioning tub all weekend and next week too. If Gail could fix the problem, Janet would be elated not to deal with her landlord at all. She felt better already. "I'll agree, but only if you let me cook dinner for you to thank you."

"Now that's an offer I can't refuse."

Janet could hear the smile in Gail's voice. "Good, then I'll see you tomorrow night," she said with a smile of her own.

CHAPTER TEN

Janet had just put the chicken in the oven to roast when the doorbell rang. Gail! Janet hurried over to the door and looked through the peephole to be sure it was her. It was, and oh did she look good standing there tall, dark, and handsome in a purple button-down shirt and jeans and holding a toolbox. *If I'm not careful, my mind will turn this into some kind of erotic fantasy involving a hot repairwoman.* Janet took a calming breath, opened the door, and smiled. "Hi." She kissed Gail lightly. Gail had a pleasant, fresh-from-the-shower soapy smell about her. "Come in."

Gail smiled and stepped in. Janet closed the door. Gail held out a bag that she had in her other hand. "I brought some just-picked vegetables to use at dinner if you want."

"Thanks." Janet accepted the bag and looked inside. "Ooh, yum!" The baby beets, arugula, and zucchini looked so appealing that she decided on the spot to cook them all tonight. The vegetables that she had already gotten at the store would have to wait. Except for the potatoes she had bought. Those were staying on the menu. Janet was going to mash them to serve with pan gravy from the roast chicken that she was preparing.

Gail took the opportunity to admire Janet's curves in her deliciously snug jeans and fitted blouse as Janet sifted through the bag of vegetables. Gail's gaze eventually found its way to the kitchen and alighted on a dish on the kitchen counter. Was that the source of the wonderful, buttery, baked aroma that she had been noticing? "Please tell me we're eating whatever that is."

Janet looked up from the bag and turned to follow Gail's gaze. "Yes, we most definitely are. That's dessert." She smiled. "There was a display of early peaches at the grocery store, so I bought some and made a peach crisp."

"Mmm. I'm so glad."

Janet laughed. "I'm glad you brought an appetite." She walked into the kitchen and set the bag of vegetables on the counter. She took the baby beets out of the bag and glanced over at Gail. "Don't you want to set down your toolbox?"

"I can, but I thought I'd go ahead and take care of the bathtub drain first." Gail didn't like to think of Janet having to wait days on end with a broken drain until her landlord got around to having a plumber come over.

"Oh, good idea!" Janet paused with the bundle of arugula in her hand. "I was so busy thinking of what I can make with these beautiful vegetables that I'd almost forgotten." She set the arugula down.

"No worries. I'm glad you like them."

"Oh, I do. And that bathtub I've been fighting with is right this way." Janet led the way to the bathroom, stopping in the doorway and gesturing to the tub.

Gail walked in and set her toolbox on the floor. The tub was empty now, so any water must have eventually drained out. Gail stepped into the tub and surveyed the drain setup. It looked straightforward enough.

Janet leaned against the doorway, watching.

"No pressure, right?" Gail asked with a smile.

"Oh, sorry. Am I making you nervous?"

"Nah, I've got this. I was only kidding." Gail reached for a screwdriver and a rag from her toolbox. She knelt in the tub to cover the drain with the rag. "As soon as I unscrew the cover plate and pull everything out, I'll have an idea of what the problem is."

"Wow, I think I've hired the right woman for the job," Janet said with a smile.

"I aim to please." Gail smiled back.

Janet laughed. "I better keep up my end of the bargain then and get back to preparing dinner."

Janet returned to the baby beets and arugula on the kitchen counter. She needed to get those baby beets in the oven, as they'd need time to roast and cool before she used them in a salad with the arugula. They were small enough and fresh enough that it was doable. She trimmed and scrubbed them, wrapped them in foil, and placed them in the oven with the chicken.

Now…what else to put on the salad? Janet had some goat cheese in the refrigerator that would work. And maybe she could add some nuts to the salad. Walnuts! Candied walnuts! Janet could make her grandma's candied walnuts for the salad. If Gail loved the cookies, she would love the candied walnuts too. They didn't take long to make, either, and Janet knew the recipe by heart. She got out the ingredients. It was just going to be a little tricky with everything else that she was cooking because the nuts cooked first on the stove and then in the oven, but she wanted to treat Gail to a nice dinner.

Gail inhaled the wonderful smells drifting from the kitchen as she worked. She swallowed against the extra saliva pooling in her mouth and focused on her task. She inspected the linkage that she had removed from the hole behind the cover plate in the bathtub. One of the connections on the linkage was slightly tangled up on itself. Not good. She untangled the linkage, and it hung straight, but looked worn and fragile. Gail worried that Janet would have the same problem in the bathtub again without a new part. It was a very common problem, which is why Gail had swung by the hardware store on the drive over this evening and bought a new linkage to have at the ready.

Gail installed the new linkage and assessed its fit by running some water and then flipping the drain lever. She wanted the tub to work as well as it could for Janet. She adjusted the linkage a little more so that the drain lever could achieve a better seal and did another test. Perfect! Janet would be all set to take comfortable baths. Gail put her tools away and set her toolbox aside.

She went in search of Janet in the kitchen and was met with the sight of Janet skillfully tossing sliced zucchini in a skillet like a celebrity chef. Gail had tried that once, and half of the vegetables in the pan had flown out and landed on the stove. There was a gorgeously brown whole roast chicken on a platter. And was that a pot of mashed potatoes nearby? Janet was now stirring something with a whisk in a roasting pan on the stove. Was she making gravy? Yum! Gail hadn't had homemade gravy in eons.

"It smells fantastic in here!" Gail said as she walked into the kitchen.

Janet glanced up from pouring the gravy from the roasting pan into a small pot and smiled. "Thanks."

"And I'm pleased to announce that the bathtub drain is fixed."

"That's wonderful! Thank you so much!" Janet turned to hug her. "I'm so impressed that you know how do that."

"You're very welcome." Gail was proud of the repair skills she had acquired over the years and even more pleased by Janet's praise. "Need any help in here?" Gail could hardly wait to eat. Everything looked so, so good.

"No, I'm just putting on the finishing touches. Why don't you have seat? Oh, but first let me get us some wine." Janet reached into the refrigerator and produced a bottle of white wine.

"Want me to open it?" Gail asked.

"Sure."

As Gail opened the wine, she watched Janet reach into the refrigerator once more and get two little plates of something out. Gail thought she saw arugula, so maybe it was salad. Salad sounded good too. Gail poured the wine into the glasses and took a seat.

Janet brought the plates over and joined Gail at the table.

Gail's eyes widened in delight at the plate of salad before her. Janet had turned her arugula and beets into this beautiful salad, complete with candied walnuts and cheese.

Janet raised her glass and looked at Gail. "Here's to being able to soak in the bath and drain the tub afterward. Thank you again." Janet gave her a big smile.

Gail clinked glasses with Janet and smiled back. "You're welcome again. Feel free to break the drain anytime, because I can tell that is going to be a wonderful dinner." Gail forked up a bite of salad, making sure to get a little piece of each of the ingredients, and ate. Oh, it was delicious. The beets were cooked perfectly, and the vinaigrette Janet had dressed the salad with really complemented the arugula. The dots of goat cheese were nice and creamy, and the candied walnuts were amazing with their maple and vanilla flavors. "God, this is delicious. Do you cook like this often?"

"What do you mean?"

"All of these different things?"

Janet smiled. "Only when a hot repairwoman brings me a bag of vegetables." She made a show of letting her eyes roam over Gail's body. Gail felt every trace of her gaze as it caressed her face, danced across her shoulders, and then lingered on her breasts. Her nipples tightened. She was tempted to get up, take Janet in her arms, and kiss her soundly, but doing that in the middle of this splendid dinner didn't seem like the right time. She cleared her throat. "I didn't mean for you to cook the whole bag of vegetables tonight."

Janet shrugged. "They looked so fresh and lovely that I couldn't resist. I had the time since the chicken was basically cooking itself in the oven."

Gail laughed. She raised her glass again. "Well, here's to self-cooking chickens."

Janet laughed and tapped her glass to Gail's glass. "But to answer your question, I eat away from home all the time when I'm traveling for work, and it's not always food that I want or enjoy, so when I'm home I cook things that I like. I don't usually cook this many things at once, but tonight I was inspired." Janet's eyes focused on Gail's eyes, and one side of her mouth turned up in a playful grin.

Gail felt herself blush. She smiled back.

When they were done with the salads, Janet took their empty plates into the kitchen. "Okay, which pieces of chicken would you like?" Janet asked, a knife in one hand and a large fork in the other.

"I think I'd like a thigh and some of the breast," Gail said.

"That's easy enough." Janet began carving.

Gail watched as Janet filled their plates. Her mouth was watering again.

Janet brought the plates over and rejoined Gail at the table.

"Wow, this looks absolutely delicious." Gail could tell from the golden-brown skin of the chicken that the meat was going to be utterly succulent. She cut into the tender, moist meat. "Mmm, this chicken is fantastic!"

"I'm really glad you're enjoying dinner." Janet smiled at her and took a bite of chicken.

"I am." Gail spooned up some of the mashed potatoes and gravy. So good. She next ate some of the zucchini. She always enjoyed zucchini prepared simply like this, with only salt and pepper, but there was something extra that Janet did that just made things…better. "So, tell me about your dance lesson. I didn't get a chance to ask you about it last night on the phone."

Janet's eyes lit up. "It was fun, and we had a really good instructor, a college student. Her name's Natalie. She taught us a dance called Flying Eights."

"That's a fun one." Gail took a sip of wine.

"Yeah. It was fast, but it was easy for me to pick up after our night of dancing at The Pink Stallion."

"That's great!"

Janet nodded. "Natalie thought private lessons might be better for me and offered to teach me after the other class."

That gave Gail pause. Her mind started to churn as she wondered about this Natalie and her "private lessons."

"Are you going to take them?" Gail asked, trying to keep her voice neutral.

"Yes. I think I'll be able to learn faster that way. I have my first private lesson next week."

Gail nodded. She was glad Janet had found lessons that she was excited about but wasn't thrilled that she was going to be taking one-on-one lessons with some woman, probably a cute young woman, no less. Why couldn't it be some guy, preferably a gay guy?

Gail made an effort to push her negative thoughts away and to refocus on the delicious dinner before her. She couldn't remember the last time that someone had cooked for her. Usually, dates liked to be taken out to dinner. That was fine of course, but there was something so much more intimate about a home-cooked meal.

Janet liked watching Gail eat. She ate with relish. Janet had had more than one girlfriend who ate in such a careful, timid way that it took the pleasure out of meals. She could tell that Gail enjoyed food, and Janet loved having someone like that to cook for.

Gail had cleaned her plate. "I'd ask for seconds but I'm saving room for that peach crisp." She fixed her eyes on the dish on the counter.

Janet laughed. "Peach crisp, coming right up." She cleared their empty plates and silverware and then set about serving the peach crisp. She spooned out a generous portion for Gail and a slightly smaller one for herself.

She sat back down to enjoy the dessert.

"Oh, yeah. This tastes every bit as buttery and peachy as I had dreamed," Gail said.

Janet was glad the early peaches from the grocery store were flavorful. She'd made a terrible crisp with early peaches once.

Gail sat back after finishing her serving of peach crisp. "I am officially full. What a fantastic meal."

"I'm so glad you liked it. Let me put away the leftovers, and then maybe we can go into the living room and see if anything good is on TV." She took their dishes into the kitchen.

"Okay. Let me help with cleanup." Gail pushed back her chair and stood up. She joined Janet in the kitchen and began filling the sink with soap and hot water, adding the dirty pots and pans.

Janet wanted to protest since Gail was her guest, but they would be able to sit on the couch sooner if she had a little help in the kitchen. And she very much wanted to sit with Gail on the couch, have Gail maybe put her arm around her, lean close, kiss her.

Spending time in the kitchen with Gail was nice too, though, so there was no rush. Janet hadn't had a woman in her apartment since moving from Connecticut, and doing these simple tasks in the kitchen with Gail made her apartment feel more like a home. Janet dried the roasting pan, skillet, baking sheet, and other items as Gail handed them to her after washing and rinsing. Janet put the other dishes in the dishwasher and put away the leftover food.

Kitchen tidied, she poured the remains from the wine bottle into their glasses and handed Gail's glass to her. "Let's go see what's on TV." She led Gail to the front room and turned on the TV with the remote.

Gail sat down next to Janet on the couch. Sitting this close to Janet in the intimacy of the apartment was already making Gail's blood hum. She sipped her wine and tried to calm herself by watching the channels go by as Janet searched for something to watch. It wasn't working. She couldn't continue sitting this close to Janet without doing something with her hands, and she didn't want to start pawing Janet like a teenager. She set down her wine and got up.

Janet gave her a curious glance but didn't question her as she went into the kitchen.

Gail picked up a pump bottle of lotion that she had noticed near the kitchen sink while she was doing dishes. She came back to the couch and sat down with it.

"What's that for?" Janet asked.

"I thought I could give you a foot rub."

Janet tilted her head in a question.

"Didn't you say that your feet get sore from your new boots?" Gail asked.

Janet nodded. "Yeah, but it's not as bad anymore. There's no need for you to go to the trouble to rub them. You've already helped me so much by fixing the bathtub stopper."

"It was no problem. I was glad to do that for you. And I know that getting sore feet from breaking in boots is no fun."

"Well, a foot rub does sound nice…" Janet was smiling. "Are you sure it's no trouble?"

"No trouble at all," Gail said. "Just give me your feet, and I'll have them feeling better in no time." She pumped some of the lotion into her hands and made a show of getting ready by rubbing them briskly.

Janet laughed. She set down the remote and her wineglass and started slipping off her shoes and socks.

Gail glanced at the TV. It had ended up on a home improvement channel that she sometimes watched, but she didn't think she would be paying much attention to it tonight.

Janet brought her legs up on the couch, lying back against the cushions and extending one leg toward Gail.

Gail gently grasped Janet's leg. Janet's calf was nicely toned, and Gail couldn't help wondering what the rest of her leg felt like. *Maybe this wasn't the best idea for something to distract me.* She brought Janet's foot to rest in her lap so that she could start the massage. "You have cute toes," Gail said.

Janet smiled and blushed.

Gail held Janet's foot in both hands and began the massage with light, gliding strokes and a few squeezes with her hands up and down Janet's foot to get a good circulation started.

Janet relaxed into the couch and sighed appreciatively.

Gail began rubbing the ball of Janet's foot with her thumbs, starting at the base of her big toe then working her way along the other toes.

"Mmm. That feels so good," Janet said. "And your hands are nice and warm."

"I'm glad you're enjoying it." Gail moved her fingers to Janet's big toe and gently squeezed up the length of it. She squeezed Janet's other toes in turn. She gazed at Janet reclined on the couch. Janet's head was back, and her eyes were closed now. Gail shifted on the couch cushions. She wanted to trail kisses over the curve of Janet's neck. *No. Focus. Focus on the massage.* She used her thumbs to work her way down the length of Janet's foot from her toes to her heel.

Janet moaned softly.

Oh, God. Did Janet make those kinds of moans in bed? Gail felt a stirring in her groin. *I need to get a hold of myself. It's only a foot massage.* She grasped Janet's heel in one hand and began using the thumb of her other hand to make a small circle with gentle pressure in one area of her heel. She then moved her thumb to a new area and made more small circles.

Janet moaned softly again, seeming unaware of the intermittent sounds of pleasure escaping her mouth. Gail's groin was starting to pulse with each new moan from Janet. She took a fortifying breath and finished rubbing all sides of Janet's heel. She then massaged her Achilles tendon and ankle area and rotated her foot gently around a few times.

When Gail began kneading Janet's arch with her thumbs, Janet let out an "Ohhh..." that made Gail's hands falter for a moment at a particularly strong pulse of her groin. *I don't know if I can handle massaging the other foot.* She recovered as best she could and continued kneading. Gail used the backs of her fingers and her knuckles to briskly slide the length of Janet's foot to let her know she was done with that foot. Gail took another fortifying breath before saying, "Okay, give me your other foot."

Lethargically, Janet asked, "What? Oh. Okay." She extended her other foot and brought her first leg back.

Gail pumped more lotion into her hands. She did her best to repeat the movements of the massage on Janet's other foot while Janet continued making those luscious noises and arching back into the couch cushions. "Okay, you're all done." Gail released Janet's foot.

Janet stretched luxuriously, raising her arms and squeezing her eyes shut briefly before reopening them in a half-lidded gaze. "My feet feel wonderful. Thank you so much."

Gail cleared her throat. "You're welcome." She needed a moment to collect herself, so she gently moved Janet's foot from her lap and stood up.

Janet's brow furrowed slightly.

"Let me go wash this extra lotion off my hands." Gail walked into the kitchen. She rested her hands on the sink and took some fortifying breaths. She felt so swollen that it was distracting. *I think I should leave now before I carry her off to bed.* She washed the lotion from her hands and then dried her hands and walked back into the living room.

Janet glanced up as Gail came back into the room. Why had Gail stopped way over there instead of coming back to the couch? Janet straightened from her reclined position. "You don't have to leave yet, do you?"

"Um..." Gail shifted on her heels.

As far as Janet was concerned, the evening was just getting started. "Don't you want to sit back down with me?"

"I do, but..." Gail shrugged.

Janet was sure that Gail wanted her as much as she wanted Gail, but something seemed to be holding Gail back. Janet clicked off the TV. "I have a question."

Gail shifted her feet again. "Yes?"

"That thing you said to me a few weeks ago, after Tina's party, about your intentions being good?"

Gail tilted her head. "Yeah?"

Janet brought her fingers to her own blouse and undid a button while she gazed at Gail, her pulse pounding loudly in her ears. She slowly caressed her own skin around and below the opening of her blouse collar, keeping her eyes on Gail.

Gail's eyes widened and followed Janet's fingers.

Janet undid another button. "Your intentions weren't *all* good, were they?"

Gail opened her mouth, but no reply came out. Janet continued undoing the buttons of her blouse. Gail licked her lips.

"Because I want to feel your hands on the rest of my body." Janet swallowed, a little shocked at herself.

Gail finally found her voice. "I don't want you to think I massaged you with the idea of getting you into bed."

"I don't think that." Janet undid the second to last button. "What I think is...I want you to kiss me." She undid the last button, stood up, and let her shirt fall open to reveal her breasts nestled in a lacey bra.

Gail's eyes darkened with desire, and Janet's nipples hardened against the fabric of her bra. Gail stepped to her and brushed the blouse open further, trailing her hands down Janet's torso until they rested on the sides of her waist.

Janet's eyes fluttered closed for a moment at the sensation of Gail's warm fingers on her bare skin. At a small movement of Gail's thumbs on her abdomen, Janet trembled with anticipation.

Gail regarded her intently, and Janet met her heated gaze. Gail's hands slid up and across her back until Gail's arms enveloped her in a firm embrace. Gail dipped her head to meet Janet's lips, kissing her with an intensity that took her breath away and left her feeling pleasantly light-headed.

"Was that the kind of kiss you wanted?" Gail breathed.

"Yes," Janet managed to say. "That and more." Janet leaned nearer, and Gail claimed her mouth again. Gail moved her hands to either side of Janet's breasts and thumbed her hard nipples through the material of the bra. Janet moaned as Gail continued, her legs weakening as Gail caressed her. She needed to do this lying down. She broke the kiss and began undoing the buttons to Gail's shirt, stepping backward to pull Gail in the direction of the bedroom. Somehow, they managed to get into the room. Janet stopped them near the bed and pushed Gail's unbuttoned shirt off her shoulders. Gail shrugged out of the shirt and tossed it aside.

Janet breathed in at the sight of Gail's fit torso with shapely breasts in a plain bra over a flat stomach. She stepped forward to run her hands over Gail's shoulders and felt the movement of the muscles as Gail reached to remove the blouse still covering Janet. Janet wriggled out of it and set it aside, standing before Gail in only her jeans and lace bra. Holding Gail's gaze, Janet undid her bra and slipped it off.

"You're so beautiful," Gail said.

Janet loved the sincerity in Gail's eyes.

Gail bent and kissed Janet's breasts, running her tongue around one of the taut nipples while rubbing the palm of her hand lightly over the other. The sensations were driving Janet wild. She moaned. Gail guided her onto the bed, and Janet reached to unfasten Gail's bra. She wanted to see and feel Gail's breasts too. Gail shrugged out of the bra and Janet reached for them, palming them. They were lovely and full, the nipples tight and peaked. She lightly thumbed Gail's stiff nipples, earning a groan.

Janet moved her arms around Gail and pulled Gail down to her for a kiss. As the kiss deepened, Janet raised her hips, seeking more contact with Gail.

Gail broke the kiss, breathing fast. "Let's get the rest of our clothes out of the way." Her face was flushed, her brown eyes dark.

"Good idea," Janet said. "I want to feel all of you against me. And the quicker, the better." She shed her jeans and panties while Gail did the same. Then Janet reached for her, and Gail lowered herself on top, kissing her. Janet reveled in the sensation of Gail's breasts against her own, Gail's pelvis against her own.

Gail looked into her eyes. "I want you so much," she murmured, now kissing along Janet's neck. "The sounds that you were making out there during that foot massage were driving me wild."

Janet's hands on Gail's back stilled for a moment as she realized what she might have sounded like. "Oh, I didn't mean to…"

"No, don't be embarrassed. That's not what I meant at all." Gail raised up from where she had been kissing and running her tongue along Janet's neck. "I like hearing those sounds out of you, of you experiencing pleasure. And I really like being the cause of them."

Janet's embarrassment faded, and she smiled. Gail already made her feel so special, so much more cherished than any other woman ever had. She hugged Gail to her. "I like you being the cause of them too."

"Good. So don't hold back—I want to hear you." Gail resumed kissing and licking at the sensitive flesh of Janet's neck, making Janet moan and clutch Gail's shoulders.

"Yeah, like that," Gail said. Gail kissed along her collarbone.

"Mmm." Janet arched her neck and moved one of her hands into Gail's soft hair. Gail moved down to tease Janet's nipples with her mouth and hands. The little squeezes and licks consumed Janet with need. She brought Gail's face up for another deep kiss and then released her from the kiss. "I want you inside me."

"I want that too." Gail repositioned herself and reached one hand down as she resumed placing kisses on Janet's torso. Gail trailed her hand along Janet's thigh, moving her fingers gradually inward. At the feel of Gail's fingers meeting her moist heat, Janet's breath caught. Gail trailed her fingers through Janet's slick folds, and Janet moaned. As Gail eased inside her, Janet arched into her fingers, enjoying the sensation of Gail filling her. Gail began a steady rhythm, just like Janet needed at this moment. Janet's breathing became rapid as Gail pumped in and out. Gail brought her thumb up to bump Janet's clit with the strokes, and Janet's rapid breathing became mingled with passionate cries. Janet was desperate, but she didn't want this to end. A tingle began in the tips of her toes, working its way up through her legs, her arms, her breasts, centering itself as Gail's fingers moved faster, harder, deeper, until Janet cried out with a final moan of release. She held on to Gail as she recovered her breath. "Oh my God, that was just how I needed it right now."

Gail shifted slightly and kissed Janet. Janet felt Gail's wet center brush against her leg. She reached a hand down to cup Gail, finding her very swollen. "You are so wet. I did that?"

"Are you kidding, a few more sounds from you, and I think I could have come from that alone," Gail said helplessly.

"Hmm," Janet said, turning to move on top of her. Gail must be in as much desperate need as she had been just moments ago. "I wanted to take my time with your body, but I have a feeling that quicker attention might be appreciated right now."

When Gail managed a nod, Janet trailed kisses down her torso until she arrived at the heat between Gail's thighs. She intended to satisfy Gail as much as Gail had satisfied her. Janet dipped her tongue in Gail's silky wet folds, and Gail groaned. Janet couldn't help a smile at Gail's ecstatic sound but kept her tongue moving. As Janet traced and lightly sucked at the swollen flesh, Gail clutched at the bedsheets. Janet tongued Gail's swollen clit, and Gail's hips surged. Janet knew it wouldn't take much more to push Gail over the edge. She began circling and flicking with her tongue, and Gail's hips soon arched. "Oh, yes! God, Janet, yes!" Gail cried.

As Gail's body relaxed, Janet rested her head against her thigh for a moment. She was glad to give Gail the quick release she had needed after unwittingly torturing her with her moans during the foot massage. There would be plenty of time to go slow later. Janet moved up the bed to lay next to Gail. "Better?" Janet asked Gail with a smile.

"Amazing," Gail breathed. Gail's face had a blissful expression on it, and Janet liked being the one who put it there. Janet kissed her before lying down beside her.

Gail put her arm around her, and Janet moved closer.

"Now that I think about it," Janet said, "I guess I kind of threw myself at you out there tonight—unbuttoning my blouse and all that—but I really didn't want you to leave."

Gail turned to her and smiled. "If you're waiting for me to complain, it's not going to happen. I'm so glad you talked me into staying." She gave Janet a gentle kiss.

Janet smiled and kissed her back. "I've wanted you since we went dancing. You looked so hot that night, I could barely remember my own name."

Gail looked at her, clearly relishing the compliment. "Oh yeah?"

"Yeah," Janet said.

Gail smiled. "You looked pretty hot yourself." She raised herself onto an elbow and kissed Janet again. After the kiss, she idly traced the fingers of one hand along the skin of Janet's abdomen. "I almost made a move that night. I think I would have, if you were anyone else." Gail paused, and Janet sensed that Gail was gearing up to say something important. "But I didn't make a move because I had the sense that we could have something more than just a casual encounter." She searched Janet's face.

Janet regarded her warmly and waited. She had felt that potential for more also. It was obvious to Janet from the start that Gail was a sensitive and caring woman, the kind of woman she could see a future with.

"I've been enjoying spending time with you," Gail continued, "first at the party, then dancing, then at my farm, and now here at your apartment. It's been nice to take things kind of slow. Well, not all that slow, really." Gail chuckled. "But you know what I mean."

Janet smiled. "Yeah, I know what you mean. I'm glad you feel that way. I feel that way about us too." She pulled Gail closer for a kiss.

After a moment, Gail let out a sigh. "But I have to admit, I'm still afraid of getting hurt again in a relationship."

Janet propped herself up to look Gail in the eyes. She clasped one of Gail's hands in her own. "I've never been a cheater, so you don't need to worry about that from me." Gail nodded, but Janet knew that Gail would probably have a hard time believing it of anyone. Janet gave her a kiss before lying back down. "Just so we're clear...I don't like to share either."

"You won't have to share me. I meant it when I said that I'm not interested in dating anyone else while I'm dating you."

"Good. That's settled, let's get some sleep." Janet realized she had assumed that Gail would stay the night. But she would stay, wouldn't she? This was no one-night stand. Just as Janet was about to ask and make sure, Gail turned onto her side to face her, draping an arm over her. Janet moved to lay on her side as well, snuggling back against Gail. Janet relaxed, and fell asleep with Gail wrapped around her.

CHAPTER ELEVEN

Janet yawned as she sat in the less-than-comfortable chair in the airport departure lounge. She had gone dancing with Gail again last night at The Pink Stallion. Even though Janet had needed to get up early the next day, she'd been eager to spend more time with Gail, especially if it meant more of the lovemaking they had done on Friday night. Janet had thought that she would be able to manage well enough if they left The Pink Stallion early. Of course, they'd had so much fun dancing that they had stayed longer than they should have. By the time they got home, it was really too late for Gail to come in, so she'd left Janet to get some sleep. But Janet had been so keyed up from their evening together that she hadn't been able to fall asleep for hours afterward.

Janet yawned again. She had lain there in bed, wishing Gail had joined her anyway, never mind the early flight. Then she had wished that she had a normal job where she didn't have to think about flight schedules interfering with dates or dance classes or other things she wanted to do. Around and around her mind had spun, and she was lucky to have gotten any sleep at all. Janet had a feeling that it was going to be a long week this week at Riverview Hospital in Idaho Falls.

Janet's phone buzzed from within her purse. She fished it out. "Hello?"

Aaron's voice greeted her. "The CEO at Riverview emailed me yesterday that he moved your meeting with himself and the CFO up an hour. He must have meant to email you."

"What? It was scheduled tight as it was!" Janet rubbed her dry, aching eyes. "I hope he realizes the airline won't fly me there faster just because they moved the meeting."

"I know, but I told him you could do it. I know you haven't worked with them yet since it was the previous manager who did their startup, but you know they've been dissatisfied with the pharmacy department's performance. I want to keep them happy so that we don't lose the account."

Aaron had indeed mentioned the complaints to her. Janet also knew from her communication with the hospital's Director of Pharmacy that the hospital administrators were very demanding. "Why was the CEO emailing on Sunday anyway?"

"I don't know, but I think he and the CFO play golf together. Maybe they decided it then."

Janet groaned. To get to the meeting on time now, she was really going to have to hoof it off the plane to the car rental counter and hope there wasn't a huge line, and she was going to have no chance of eating lunch. After finishing the phone call with Aaron, she went in search of a shop in the airport to buy some energy bars or something else that would be convenient to eat while driving to her meeting. Now she really did regret not spending the night with Gail. At least then she would have had some more nice memories to sustain her this week.

* * *

Gail's morning had been hectic, and she was looking forward to sitting down for a few minutes for lunch. There had been a scheduled pickup of a shipment of walnuts, but the truck driver had arrived two hours early, before Gail's workers were even there yet. Gail had had to go get a forklift from another location on the farm, drive it down the road while morning commuters zoomed around her, and then load the pallets of boxes into the trailer herself.

Gail opened her refrigerator and pulled out a plate of leftover chicken with mashed potatoes and gravy from her dinner with Janet a few nights ago. It was especially nice to have today, when Janet was out of town. Gail missed her already, and having leftovers of the meal they had shared together was comforting.

Gail took her food outside and sat at the patio table. Bo immediately bounded up and plopped his head into her lap, looking up at her with his big brown eyes. She tried not to encourage bad habits by feeding him from the table, but he looked so cute and pitiful that she gave him a bite of chicken anyway. "Taste this, Bo. My girlfriend made it for me." *Girlfriend. It's been a long time since I've had occasion to use that word. It sounds nice.*

Bo gobbled down the chicken and peered up at her for more.

"It's good, isn't it?" She gave him just a little more of her lunch.

Gail wondered how Janet was doing. She was probably tired. Gail hadn't meant to keep her out so late last night, but they always had such a good time together. And it had been hard to leave her at the apartment last night, when what Gail wanted to do was climb into bed and make love all night. But they had both needed to get some rest before work, especially Janet.

Gail went back into her house for the dish of leftover peach crisp for dessert. She spooned out a serving, heated it a little in the microwave, and dug in. No way was she sharing this with Bo.

* * *

Janet lay in bed in her chain hotel near the airport, waiting to fall asleep, but thoughts of her unpleasant meeting earlier that day with the CEO and administrators at Riverview Hospital were keeping her awake. The CEO and CFO had repeatedly spoken of wanting to reduce pharmacy costs. Apparently, both men expected an instantaneous turnaround of the financial performance of the pharmacy the moment they contracted with Rockland. Janet had seen the numbers there before the Rockland contract and knew there was room for improvement but also knew that improvement would take time. She had tried to adjust administration's expectations accordingly.

Three nights here was going to seem endless. Not that the hotel was unpleasant; it was new and clean and as comfortable as any place else she stayed. But she wanted to be back in Danforth, wanted to see Gail. She wanted to be in her own bed, wanted Gail to be with her in bed again. She wanted to feel Gail's warm lips, wanted to feel her touch, wanted to…

Janet sighed. She wasn't going to fall asleep any time soon.

She threw off the covers and got out of bed. She paced for a moment, thinking…about Gail, about their relationship, about what she could possibly do to help herself fall asleep… She paused. It was a little daring, but then didn't a new relationship involve risk? She went to her purse on the table and rummaged around in it until she found her cell phone. Then she stripped out of her pajamas. She picked up her phone again, scrolled to Gail's number, pressed it, put the phone on speaker, and set it on the nightstand. She got back in bed while the phone rang on the other end.

"Hello?" Gail's voice sounded a little sleepy.

"Hi, it's me. I'm not calling too late, am I?"

"No, I'm still up."

"Good. I didn't want to wake you, but I was thinking of you."

"You were?"

"Yes." Janet paused. "I'm in bed. Naked."

"Oh?" Gail's voice was husky.

"Yes, I was thinking about your kisses and your hands and how you would be touching me if I were there with you." A moment passed. "Gail?"

"Yes?"

"Make love to me."

"But…you're in Idaho."

"Tell me what would you do."

"Oh." She cleared her throat. "Well…I would kiss you."

"Kiss me where?"

"First, I would kiss your lips. I've been thinking about those soft lips of yours, and I've been longing to kiss them again. And again. Several times."

"I love your kisses." Janet closed her eyes. Her lips parted of their own accord as she imagined Gail kissing her.

"Then I make the kisses long and slow and deep," Gail said.

Janet's chest tightened with desire. "It feels good," she breathed.

"I work my way down your neck. Lots of kisses there."

Janet moaned. "I can feel your lips against my throat." She arched her neck against her pillow.

"At the pulse in your neck, I pause to use my tongue."

Janet moaned again.

"Now I'm kissing your breasts."

"You're making me so wet."

"How wet?" Gail asked huskily. "Dip your hand down and tell me."

Janet felt her own slickness. "Really wet."

"Good. I like you really wet."

Janet's fingers brushed her clit. She drew in a sudden breath.

"Don't get ahead of me. I'm not done with your breasts," Gail scolded her.

Janet let out a whimper, but brought her hand back up.

"Now, pretend your hands are my hands. Put your hands on your breasts and feel me there. Feel me cup and caress your breasts."

"Mmm, I do. You're making my nipples so hard," Janet said. She longed for Gail to take each of her hard nipples in her mouth in turn and lavish them with attention.

"Feel the little squeezes my fingers give your hard nipples."

Janet squeezed her nipples and hummed in pleasure.

"That's right," Gail encouraged. "Now feel my fingers as they slide down your abdomen to those golden curls of yours."

Janet moved her hand down. "Oh…"

"Can you feel my fingers move across your wetness?"

"Oh, yes. Yes, I feel you." Janet knew that her breathing was getting loud and fast but she couldn't control it.

"Tell me what my hands are doing to you."

"You're stroking me," Janet panted. "Stroking me with your fingers, stroking through my wetness."

"Are my fingers making you feel good?" Gail breathed.

"Yes, oh, you feel so good." Janet stroked a little faster now, listening to Gail's breaths on the other end of the line. "You're stroking me up and down, up and around, stroking my hard clit with your fingers."

"Do you want to come?"

"Yes, make me come, stroke me harder, oh you feel so good, you're going to make me come…" Janet cried out in release, waves of pleasure rolling through her. Afterward, she lay still, enjoying the blissful feeling, until she realized that Gail had gone quiet. She sat up. "Gail? Are you still there?"

Gail's response was incoherent.

"Gail? Are you okay?"

"Yeah. Or, I will be after a cold shower." Gail chuckled. "But actually, it's my cell phone that you should be worried about. I was squeezing it so hard that I think I almost cracked it."

"Oh, no." Janet laughed. She paused. "I miss you. When I get back, I'll take care of you, don't you worry."

* * *

Janet looked out over Utah from her window seat. After the layover in Salt Lake City, it wouldn't be much longer before she was back in Sacramento. She wondered if Gail would be home if she drove out to the farm. Janet wasn't sure what had gotten into her to initiate phone sex. It wasn't something she had ever done with anyone. She supposed she hadn't been compelled to try it until now because there hadn't been anyone she had wanted badly enough. Janet found that she had a different, more intense level of desire when it came to Gail.

Since the flight was scheduled to get in at noon, Janet thought that she should have time to squeeze in a visit to Gail's before tonight's line dance lesson. But between the time needed for collecting her luggage and driving out to Gail's, and then leaving to fit in a meal, change her clothes, and get to her lesson, it would have to be a short visit. Janet hoped that Gail would be pleasantly surprised if she drove out to give her a personal thank-you for responding so gamely to her phone call the other night.

"What would you like to drink, miss?" Janet heard the voice of the flight attendant.

Janet turned her gaze from the window. "Just water, please."

"And for you, sir?" the flight attendant asked Janet's seatmate, a nicely dressed man with graying hair.

"Water for me too," he said.

Knowing that it was unlikely the flight attendant would include a snack with the drink, Janet rummaged in her purse for the leftover candied walnuts she'd packed.

"I see you came prepared," Janet's seatmate said.

"Always!" Janet opened the bag and set it on her tray table.

He eyed the bag of walnuts. "I think it's terrible that the airlines don't hand out nuts with the drinks anymore. I used to love the honey peanuts."

That was a hint if Janet ever heard one. "These are candied walnuts. Would you like some?"

"Thanks, if you have enough to share." He unfolded the napkin that the flight attendant had given him with his drink and placed it on his tray table. Janet poured a small pile of nuts from the bag onto it.

"Mmm, these are good," he said. "These are really quite addictive, Ms. ..."

"Webber, but call me Janet."

"Pleased to meet you, Janet. I'm William Hewitt. Tell me, did you make these nuts?"

"Mm-hmm."

"Are you a chef?"

She swallowed. "You flatter me—no, just a home cook."

"I can tell that there is maple syrup in here. So much more flavorful than plain sugar or corn syrup. And the coating is not too thick."

This guy is quite a critic.

"You could sell these, if you wanted to, I reckon."

Janet cocked her head. This was the second time that she'd been told she could sell something she'd made. First with her walnut bar cookies and now her candied walnuts. It was an interesting idea.

"You should consider it," he said, popping some more nuts into his mouth. "There are grants for that kind of thing. I work for the USDA, so I should know."

"Really? What do you do?" She always met such interesting people flying into the state capitol.

"I work in Rural Development in one of the Idaho offices, but I have business in Sacramento today. Political stuff at the capitol that I won't bore you with. Let me tell you about the grant." He leaned toward her. "The National Institute of Food and Agriculture has a grant available this month that would be right up your alley. If I remember correctly, it's something along the lines of new market opportunities for specialty crops—of which nuts are one, my dear—through small business start-up."

Janet raised her eyebrows. "That's an interesting idea, but starting a business seems like a major undertaking."

"It's actually quite simple. You can even do it online. A grant takes a lot of the financial risk out of it. I've known several people who have done it successfully."

Janet blinked. William was convincing. "You've given me something to contemplate. Maybe I'll look into it all when I get home and learn more." Janet sat back and sipped her water, thinking. Sitting next to William was fortuitous; maybe the universe was trying to tell her something. Maybe she *should* really look into this whole grant business when she got home and learn more about it.

CHAPTER TWELVE

Gail sat at her desk in the farm office, signing the last of a stack of employee payroll checks that Maria had printed out for her, when her phone buzzed in her pocket. Gail took it out and looked at the display. Janet! "Hello?"

"Hi, it's me. Are you free?" Janet sounded a little breathless.

"I can be. Is everything all right?" Gail asked.

"Everything's fine. I just...I'm back in town, and I thought I would stop by in case you were home. I probably should have called first."

"You're at the house?"

"Yeah, I'm parked in the driveway. Bo is keeping me company."

"I'm at the office. I can be right over."

"Okay, but only if I'm not disrupting anything."

"No, I was just signing some checks, but I'm finishing up. I'll see you in just a few minutes." She quickly signed the last of the employee payroll checks.

Maria came over to collect them. "Was that Janet?" she asked with a smile.

"How did you know?"

"Just a hunch—you always sound happy when you talk to her."

Gail smiled back. "She does make me happy."

"I'm glad for you. You deserve it. Now, you'd better get going so you don't keep her waiting."

Gail said goodbye to Maria and walked briskly out to her truck. It was great that Janet was back in town a little earlier than expected, but Gail hoped nothing was wrong. Janet had said she was okay, though she sounded a little anxious or maybe even excited on the phone.

 Gail pulled in next to Janet's car and got out. She took in Janet's dress slacks belted at her slim waist, her fitted blouse, and her necklace. "I've never seen you in your work clothes. You look really nice."

"Thanks," Janet replied. "I *have* seen you in your work clothes, and you look really nice too." She looked Gail up and down.

Gail grinned.

Janet put her arms around Gail's neck and kissed her. She didn't let up, continuing the kiss until Gail welcomed her inside her mouth. Janet stroked her tongue with her own, and Gail groaned at the pleasure of it. Janet seemed to have found a direct path to her center, and Gail's juices began to flow freely. Gail broke away to ask thickly, "Do you have any idea what you're doing to me?"

Janet had a playful gleam in her eye. "I'm keeping my promise." Janet kissed her again.

"Your promise?" Gail was finding it hard to think. Her gaze dropped to Janet's blouse, where a bit of cleavage showed.

"Yes, my promise. I said I would take care of you when I got back. Or, was that cold shower you mentioned the other night enough?"

"Uhh…"

"I think I can take that as a no," Janet teased. She reached for Gail's hand and began to pull her up the walkway to the house. "Maybe we should go inside where I can take care of you properly."

Gail managed to make it up the walkway and somehow unlock the door and get it open. As soon as they were inside, Janet shut the door and backed Gail up against it, resuming her deep kisses. Her hands did the rest until Gail moaned and rested against her, fulfilled.

Janet wanted to stay longer, lying in bed in Gail's arms, but she needed to get up and go home. She didn't want to be late to her first private dance lesson. She was also eager to follow up on the things that William had mentioned to her on the plane.

"You're a little quiet," Gail said. "Is everything okay?"

Janet snuggled closer. "Everything is fine. I'm just thinking about a conversation I had on the flight home. I met someone who told me I should start a business and sell candied nuts."

Gail turned onto her side to look at her. "Start a business?"

"He really liked my candied walnuts."

"They are very good. Is that something you want to do? Start a business?"

"I don't know. He said there's a grant available. The conversation got me thinking about the possibilities. It's the second time recently I've been told that I should sell my baked goods, so maybe I should give it a try. Who knows where it might lead?"

"Are you going to leave your pharmacy job?"

Janet liked that Gail was taking her idea of starting a baking business seriously. "I'm sure it would be some time before it got to the point where I could quit my day job. But yes, given the opportunity, I would leave it. I wouldn't miss it. I've been practicing pharmacy a long time. I like to think I've been good at it, but I haven't found the job particularly enjoyable. I certainly wouldn't miss my most recent job of flying all over the place to deal with administrators."

"Yeah," Gail said. She gave Janet a comforting squeeze.

"But who knows if my products would even sell?"

"I think they would. They're delicious."

"You might be slightly biased," Janet said with a smile. "I do want to look into everything, though."

"Speaking of which, Maria told me what she found out after looking into doing value-added products, like your walnut bar cookies, for the farm. Basically, it means being in the manufacturing business. I would need to build, equip, and staff a facility for that. There would be a lot of time and expense involved in getting started."

"Sounds like you should apply for a grant too," Janet joked.

Gail laughed. "Maybe. I do have the space, though, to manufacture products so building a facility on the farm would be possible. Maria also looked into renting a commercial kitchen. She found that only large equipment like ovens and mixers are provided, so people still need to bring pots, pans, utensils, and whatever else is needed. Hauling all the equipment and supplies and products back and forth all the time doesn't seem very efficient. Not only that, but there doesn't seem to be any guarantee that there will be a rental space available when it is needed, so renters may not get to make their product when they need to."

"That doesn't sound good," Janet said.

"No, renting a commercial kitchen won't work for my purposes. There is also the matter of developing recipes with my walnuts, but Maria found some companies that could do that. They will even manufacture the product for me."

"Is that something you would consider?"

"I don't really think so. I'm a farmer, and I want something as natural as possible. I know my customers do too. I liked the idea of having something homemade, like the cookies. In fact, I think I would be your first customer if you get a grant and start a business."

"You would?" Janet raised up onto an elbow.

"Definitely. I know that my CSA customers and farmers' market customers would buy walnut products, and I already know that yours are good."

"Thank you," Janet said, looking into Gail's eyes. "That's really kind of you." She reached for Gail's hand and gave it a squeeze.

"With you, it's easy," Gail said. She squeezed back.

"You realize that you're making me want you all over again," Janet said, feigning exasperation.

"What can I say? I'm a smart woman." Gail gave her a teasing smile.

Janet laughed and shook her head. "Unfortunately, I really need to get home so that I can get ready for my dance lesson with Natalie."

A frown flitted across Gail's face.

"I know," Janet said, "I'm not ready to get up either."

Janet waited in her car until the group line dance class let out of the studio. She was a little fatigued and didn't want to have to chat with her one-time classmates. Her busy day was catching up with her. She was glad that Natalie was an energetic person and hoped the energy would help revive her for the lesson.

Natalie greeted her with a friendly smile. "Hi, Janet. You're right on time."

"Yes, I've been looking forward to the lesson."

"Did you get a chance to practice at all during the week? Did your boyfriend take you to The Pink Stallion again?"

Janet sighed. *Well, here is the moment of truth. These lessons might be short-lived when Natalie finds out she has a lesbian for a private student.* "Yeah, I went to The Pink Stallion again. But my boyfriend didn't take me—my girlfriend took me. I'm gay."

"Oh," Natalie said. She blinked.

"Is that a problem for you?" Janet asked. Just how uncomfortable was Natalie going to be with her sexuality?

"What? No, no problem at all. I feel a little silly, is all. I did to you what everyone does to me—assumed you're straight." She shook her head. "When I tell my girlfriend, she'll get a good laugh at my expense."

Janet chuckled, relieved. She didn't want to have to find a new dance instructor. "Don't worry about it. I made the same assumption about you. Lesbians are the minority, after all."

"Ain't that the truth?" Natalie said with a nod. "Okay, well let's get started with a warm-up and then I'll teach you a couple of dances."

"Sounds great!"

Natalie broke the dances down into segments and had Janet practice the steps before building on with the next segment. Janet felt a little self-conscious with the instructor's full attention on her instead of spread across a group of students. The faster pace was great, though. Learning two dances was better than learning just one. And it was nice to be able to get individual help if she had trouble with a certain step.

"You're doing well," Natalie said at the end of the hour. "You have good balance, strong legs." She handed Janet a dance sheet. It had the steps Janet had just learned listed out to take home. "Use this sheet to practice the two dances, and I'll see you next week."

Janet spent Friday morning logged on to the Rockland website to finalize her reports for Aaron about the Idaho Falls account. She felt sorry for the Director of Pharmacy there who had to put up with the crazy CEO and CFO in that place on a day-to-day basis. At least Janet got to leave.

Janet took a break for lunch and then returned to her laptop to begin working on what she had been thinking about ever since her flight—grants. It took some sifting through different websites, but she found the grant that William had mentioned. Its purpose was to increase consumption of specialty crops— which Janet learned included nuts, fruits, and vegetables—by expanding women-owned businesses to create new market opportunities for food products. William was right—the grant was right up her alley.

But the deadline was the thirty-first of May, only a couple weeks away. That wasn't much time to think about all of this and decide if she wanted to take this leap into starting a business. There was so much she didn't know. She needed to gather more information.

The more she clicked through the websites, the more she saw what there was to learn. Given the limited time frame, it was all a bit overwhelming. But it did look like she could set up the business online, just like William had said. The prospect of setting up a business so easily right here and now filled her with excitement. She was getting ahead of herself, though. She didn't even yet know enough to choose the right type of business to establish from the list of choices of things like sole proprietorships and limited liability corporations. But she was now inspired enough that she knew she wanted to apply for the grant.

Janet got out her phone and called Gail. "Guess what!"

"What?" Gail asked.

"I applied for the grant!"

"Really? That's great! I hope you get it."

"Me too. It's probably a long shot, but I'm giving it a try."

"I'll keep my fingers crossed for you. When will you know if you got it?"

"The website says the recipient will be announced in July."

"That's some ways away. It's going to be tough to wait. How about I take you out to dinner tonight to celebrate your decision?"

"Okay," Janet said enthusiastically. After she and Gail made plans, Janet stood up from her chair and spontaneously danced some steps that Natalie had taught her last night, stepping and turning and scuffing and shimmying. She even threw in some slaps to her sneakers for good measure.

CHAPTER THIRTEEN

Gail hoisted a ladder out of the back of her truck and carried it into the orchard. The relatively mild spring had given way to an uncomfortably hot summer. It was with relief that Gail walked under the shady canopy of her walnut trees and into the refreshing coolness that enveloped her there. This was the very orchard she had stopped at with Janet when she had taken her on a tour of her farm in spring. Gail allowed herself a moment to savor the memory of their second kiss. She had a sudden longing to have Janet here by her side so that she could kiss her again just as she had that day.

Gail missed Janet each time she was out of town. In fact, she missed her pretty much all the time. It was hard to believe that only three months had passed since they had met at Tina and Susan's party. It was amazing how close they'd become after such a seemingly short time.

Gail walked further into the orchard. She needed to collect leaf samples to send off to the plant test lab for nutrition analysis.

She selected a tree, set up her ladder, and climbed up. She liked to do this task herself. Getting reliable test results to alert her to potential problems in her trees, such as particular nutrient deficiencies, depended on having a consistent procedure for collecting the samples from year to year. She gathered a selection of leaflets, climbed down, and put them in a paper bag.

Because she had known she was going to feel lonely today with Janet out of town, Gail had invited Tina and Susan over for dinner. They would be arriving at her house soon. Gail repeated the process of collecting leaflets from other trees until she had collected enough. She put her ladder back in the bed of the truck and drove back to her house. She needed to get cleaned up before dinner with her friends.

Gail sighed as she set the table. Maybe having Tina and Susan over tonight wasn't such a good idea after all. Seeing the two of them all cuddly together this evening was just going to remind her of Janet's absence. Gail understood that travel was part of Janet's job, but that didn't make it any easier.

The doorbell rang. Gail put a smile on her face and opened the door to greet her friends.

"It smells great in here!" Tina said, preceding Susan through the door.

"It sure does," Susan agreed.

"Thanks," Gail said, feeling a more genuine smile appear on her face. Tina and Susan were always so happy that it was infectious. "My crew picked extra tomatoes today, so I made a big pot of marinara. I hope you're in the mood for pasta."

"Fresh marinara sounds great," Tina said. She took a seat on a stool at the kitchen island, eyeing the pot on the stove.

Susan handed Gail the bottle of wine they had brought. "Do you need any help with the rest of dinner?"

"No, all that's left to do is boil the noodles, put the garlic bread in the oven, and dress the salad." Gail began opening the wine.

"Garlic bread? Yum!" Susan settled onto a stool next to Tina.

Gail smiled and set a glass of wine before each of them. She raised her glass and then clinked glasses with her two friends before taking a sip. She turned to give the marinara a stir.

"Janet is missing out," Susan said.

"Oh, she's had my tomatoes before."

"I'll bet she has," Tina said with an exaggerated waggle of her eyebrows.

"Oof!" Tina said when Susan elbowed her.

Gail shook her head at her friends' antics. Tina wasn't above the occasional juvenile joke. "What I was going to say is that I made her some bruschetta when she was here on the weekend."

"Mm-hmm, okay," Tina said, grinning from ear to ear.

"Where is she this week, anyway?" Susan asked.

"She's in Las Vegas."

"Las Vegas!" Susan's eyebrows shot up. "It's probably a hundred and ten degrees there!"

"Probably," Gail agreed. It was already hot enough here in Danforth this summer, and Las Vegas was sure to be that much worse. Janet would be facing such unbearable heat.

"At least Las Vegas isn't that far," Tina said.

"Yeah, the short flight has to be nice for her this week," Gail said. She added pasta to boiling water and put the garlic bread in the oven.

"When does Janet get back?" Susan asked.

"Thursday." Gail took a sip of her wine.

"Oh, right. She has dance lessons then." Susan sipped her wine.

"Yes, with Natalie." Gail pursed her lips, unable to hide her displeasure.

"You don't like Natalie?" Tina asked.

Gail sighed. "I don't know Natalie, but I don't like that she spends an hour dancing with my girlfriend each week."

Susan gave a laugh. "You can't think that Janet's dance teacher is a threat?"

Gail shrugged. "She *is* gay."

"Oh, come on. Don't let your imagination run away with you. They're just dance lessons. Besides, the last time we saw

Janet, didn't I hear her mention Natalie's girlfriend? Ana—wasn't that her name? So Natalie isn't even single."

"Yes, but in my experience, that doesn't always matter."

Tina shook her head. "For a lot of people, it does matter. I can't speak for Natalie, but I think it matters for Janet."

"Exactly," Susan said. "She only took the lessons because she wanted to be able to dance with you. And she was dancing really well when we all went to The Pink Stallion a couple weeks ago."

"She was, wasn't she?" Gail smiled at the memory. "She knows so many dances now."

"She does, and you must know how much she likes you. It's easy to see. Her eyes were glued to you the whole night."

Gail dropped her gaze, remembering that night. It was true, they'd had a great time, and it had continued when she and Janet had returned to Janet's apartment. Gail was a little ashamed at the admonishments from her friends.

"I just don't get a cheating vibe from Janet," Susan said, as though that settled the matter. "I think you're dwelling in the past too much, as usual."

"Maybe, but I'll be glad when the lessons with Natalie are over." Gail drained the pasta, tossed it with the marinara, and began dishing it up. Her friends were probably right. She was being ridiculous and jealous and it wasn't fair to Janet.

Janet chewed up an antacid tablet and sat down at the desk in her hotel room. The hospital administrators she had met with today had wanted to dine out for lunch on her business expense account, so lunch had been at a restaurant on the Las Vegas Strip. The food at the restaurant had tasted okay, but she'd been suffering heartburn ever since.

Janet washed down the antacid with a drink of water and turned on her laptop. A bowl of soup was probably about all she was going to be able to handle for dinner. Something summery—maybe some minestrone with tomatoes, summer squash, beans, and herbs. She started thinking about making a batch when she got home. Gail would like it also. And with Gail's vegetables, it would taste delicious.

As her relationship with Gail progressed, Janet found it harder and harder to leave each Monday morning to fly out of town. It was never easy to leave a bed that Gail was in. Gail seemed to have the magic touch, not just physically, but emotionally as well. Janet felt like she had found something special with Gail.

The hotel's Internet service was slow. While Janet waited for the browser homepage to load, she picked up the room service menu. There was broccoli cheese soup that might agree with her stomach. It was not really the kind of soup she wanted, but she decided to give it a try. She called room service and placed an order.

Now that the browser was up, she logged in to the Rockland website and replied to work emails, barely tolerating the snail's pace of the hotel Internet service. Then she logged into her personal email account. Her eyes widened when she saw what was waiting for her—an email about the grant. Could it be the announcement of the winner? She clicked.

Janet's hands fell to her lap. She sat back in her chair, crestfallen. Some woman in Ohio had won. Janet hadn't really expected to win, but it had been in the back of her mind as a possibility. She had even allowed herself to dream of leaving her draining pharmacy career and starting a little bakeshop.

Janet was still staring at her computer when there was knock on the door. Coming out of her daze, she sat up. She had all but forgotten about room service and her dinner. She got up, answered the door, and signed the bill. She sat down and took a spoonful of soup. It was a little thick, but it tasted all right. She ate on autopilot while her thoughts returned to the grant.

On the airplane, William had made getting a grant sound so easy, but of course nothing was as easy as it seemed. Maybe she shouldn't have let herself get so wrapped up in unrealistic possibilities.

Janet picked up the phone, wanting to call Gail. But at this point in their relationship she knew Gail well enough to know that she was the kind of person who might feel strongly enough about comforting her to fly to Las Vegas to do so, especially since it was only a short flight from Sacramento. The possibility of Gail doing that held great appeal, but she didn't want to impose or disrupt Gail's workweek. She set her phone back down. She would just tell her when she got back to Danforth.

Janet finished her soup and set the tray outside the door. It wasn't much dinner, but it along with the antacid seemed to have settled her stomach.

"How about some ice cream for dessert?" Gail asked.

Susan sighed and placed a hand on her stomach. "I don't know, I'm pretty full. I think I overdid it on the garlic bread."

Tina chuckled and put her arm around Susan. "Don't worry, I'll still want to kiss you later." She turned to Gail. "What kind of ice cream is it?"

"Maple walnut. Janet made it."

"Janet made it? Where does that woman find the time?"

"I don't know, but when I give her walnuts, wonderful things happen to them. She's been experimenting in her kitchen a lot ever since she applied for the grant."

"Well, I'll definitely try some of the ice cream."

"Me too," Susan said, "but maybe I'll just share with Tina."

Gail went into the kitchen and got out the big plastic tub of ice cream that Janet gave her last week.

"The winner of the grant is going to be announced soon, right?" Susan asked as Gail dished up dessert.

"Yes, it should be any time now, I think," Gail said. "I'll be really happy for her if she wins."

"Yes, wouldn't that be something if she got it?" Susan said.

Gail placed a dish of ice cream between Tina and Susan along with two spoons and sat down to enjoy her own.

"Wow, this is *so* good," Susan said.

"How do you have this in the house and not eat it all?" Tina asked.

Gail laughed. "It's not easy. Let just say it's a good thing that I burn a lot of calories on the farm."

"Janet would definitely win an ice cream making contest," Susan said.

Gail had no doubt of that.

Janet woke in a funk. The reality of not getting the grant had set in more deeply overnight. Opportunity had slipped from her grasp, and she didn't know what to do. If many of the aspects of her current job were unappealing before, they seemed doubly unappealing now. She wondered how long she could continue expending her energy taking these flights each week, staying in hotels, meeting with hospital administrators, and solving pharmacy problems. The bakeshop job she had allowed herself to fantasize about would undoubtedly also have its challenges, but surely it wouldn't be as tiresome as being Western Regional Account Manager. Even the title made her feel tired now.

Janet sighed. If she couldn't be a baker, maybe she should go back to being a Director of Pharmacy or a staff pharmacist. Not that either of those jobs were any more of a picnic than her current one, but she could at least stay in one place. She wondered how Katie was doing in her old job in Connecticut. She should give her a call and catch up.

Janet got out of bed to begin packing her luggage. At least she was booked on a good flight home today. It was a nonstop that left midmorning.

Gail sat down at her desk and shuffled through the papers there, looking for the multi-page water usage and conservation survey she had received from the county last week and that she still needed to fill out. She glanced over at Maria. "Have you seen that water survey that came in the mail?"

Maria looked around her own desk and then held a packet of papers aloft. "Yes, I have it here. I was filling out some of the sections for you." She brought the packet of papers over to Gail.

"Thanks." Gail smiled. Maria knew that getting bogged down with paperwork was not Gail's idea of fun.

Maria returned to her desk. "How the county thinks farmers have time to fill out ten pages of questions, I have no idea."

"Me neither," Gail said. She flipped to a section of the survey that Maria had left for her to fill out and began writing out answers to the questions.

Midway through, Gail took a break to check her cell phone. Why hadn't Janet called yet? Janet usually called after getting back into town. She had mentioned that the return flight would arrive shortly after noon, so she should be back. Gail considered calling her, but sometimes Janet called later if she had too many things to do when she got into town. Maybe Janet would call soon. Gail put down her phone and resumed answering the survey questions.

When Janet walked into the dance studio for her lesson, she put on a smile, but it must not have disguised her sour mood very well. Natalie started to wave hello but then gave Janet a concerned look. "Is everything okay?"

Janet considered saying that everything was fine, but she really didn't have the energy to pretend. Like a dark cloud, the disappointment of not getting the grant had continued to hang over her after she got home today. She might as well tell Natalie about it. Natalie was accustomed to hearing about some of Janet's business travails during these weekly lessons. In fact, they had gotten to know each other fairly well during these past two and a half months of dance lessons. "You know that grant I applied for? I didn't get it."

"Oh…" Natalie said. "That's got to be a major bummer."

"Yeah." Janet's shoulders slumped.

"Aw, come here," Natalie said. She stepped closer, opening her arms in invitation to give Janet a hug.

Janet took comfort in the hug, but thought she might start crying at any moment from Natalie's sympathetic embrace. She disengaged from the hug, trying to hold back tears. She gave her friend a tremulous smile. "I'm sorry. Not getting the grant is really having an effect on me."

"It's totally understandable. You had your hopes dashed."

Janet stared at the floor. "When I began thinking about the possibilities of starting a small business, it made me realize how very little I enjoy my current job."

"Yeah, I don't know how you do so much flying. It must really be tiring."

"You know what the craziest part of all this is? A couple months ago, I didn't even know I wanted a grant or to be a small business owner."

Natalie nodded sympathetically.

"Now I'm just feeling sorry for myself, and it's pathetic."

"What did Gail say when you told her?" Natalie asked.

Janet sighed. "I haven't told her yet. You're the first one I've told."

Natalie tilted her head, a little frown appearing on her forehead.

"I only found out last night when I was in my hotel," Janet continued. "I told myself that I wanted to tell Gail in person, but I think I'm mostly putting it off because I'm embarrassed. Even though the grant was probably a long shot, I kind of feel like a failure."

"Oh, don't feel that way. It would be tough to get the first grant you apply for. Maybe there's another one that you could try to get."

"Maybe." Janet didn't know if she had the energy for that.

"Well, it's something to consider," Natalie said. "In the meantime, how about we get this lesson started?"

Janet took a breath and nodded weakly. "Okay, but maybe nothing too complicated tonight. I don't think I can handle it."

"All right, I can go easy on you." Natalie gave Janet a smile, and Janet managed to give her a smile back.

Natalie turned on the music and began the instruction. Janet did her best to focus on the steps.

After the physical work of the dance lesson, Janet got into her car feeling mildly better. She looked forward to showering and getting a good night's sleep. She felt bad about not calling Gail yet, though. Time to stop procrastinating and just tell her about the grant. While Janet searched in her purse for her phone, it occurred to her that maybe she should just drive over to Gail's house and tell her in person like she had intended. She was tired but longed to see Gail after being out of town most of the week, and she looked forward to a little comfort from her girlfriend after being passed over for the grant.

Still debating, she powered on her phone. There was a missed call from Gail, making Janet feel worse about not calling. Janet typed in a text message: *Can I come over?*

Of course. Gail's texted reply came back immediately. Janet felt even worse knowing that Gail had been waiting with her phone.

Gail heard Janet's car pull into her drive. She greeted Janet at the door with a kiss and a warm hug. Releasing Janet from the embrace, she led her inside to the living room. A look at Janet's outfit of boots, jeans, and casual blouse told Gail that Janet had come straight from her line dance lesson.

Gail regarded Janet more closely as they sat on the couch. She looked as beautiful as ever, but her smile just wasn't there. Janet hadn't called when she got back in town, and now she was here looking rather serious after spending the evening at her dance lesson with Natalie. Something was obviously the matter. It crossed Gail's mind that Janet was going to break up with her. Of course, it would happen when things were going so well. Gail would be blindsided just like she had been when she had found Christine with another woman at the dance club. But this would hurt more. But what was Gail thinking? Janet gave every indication that she was happy in their relationship. Before her imagination could get any wilder, Gail lightly touched Janet's shoulder. "Are you okay?"

"I'm fine." Janet took a deep breath and let it out. "But I didn't get the grant."

"Oh, Janet, I'm sorry." Gail scooted closer to Janet and hugged her.

"Yeah, me too." Tears gathered in Janet's eyes. "I think I wanted it more than I realized. It was stupid of me to think that I could get it."

"Hey, don't say that." Gail hugged Janet closer.

Janet's tears began to flow, and she buried her head against Gail's shoulder.

"They're fools not to have given it to you." She rubbed a small circle on Janet's back while Janet cried.

Janet slowly came out of Gail's embrace. She blinked away tears, sniffling, and then sat slumped with her hands in her lap.

Gail felt helpless. Janet had wanted the grant so badly. Gail wished there were some way she could fix the situation for her, that it could be as simple as repairing a bathtub drain. She stood up and crossed the room to get a box of tissues. As she sat back down, she pulled a couple of the tissues out and handed them to Janet.

Janet dabbed at her nose. Apparently realizing the futility of dabbing, she gave it a good blow. She collapsed back against the cushions of the couch and let out a heavy sigh. "I'm just so disappointed."

Gail didn't know what other words of comfort to offer right now. "How about I start a nice, hot shower for you so that you can get cleaned up and relax?"

Janet nodded weakly.

Gail led her to the master bedroom. Janet sat down on the edge of the bed and began to lean back as if to lie down.

"Wait, let me help you with your clothes," Gail said, realizing just how exhausted her girlfriend was at the end of this day. Gail knelt before Janet and removed her boots and socks. She stood her up and unbuttoned Janet's shirt and jeans. When Janet started to help herself out of them, Gail went into the bathroom to turn on the shower to let the water heat up.

Janet looked so exhausted that Gail worried she might fall asleep in the moment that it took her start the shower. Gail reached her hand under the spray of water, testing the temperature. She turned to call, "It's ready," but she found that Janet had managed to come stand slumped against the doorway.

"I think I'm too tired to take a shower."

"I think a shower will make you feel better," Gail coaxed. She held out a hand for Janet, who accepted and got into the shower.

Janet only stood dully under the hot water, letting it rain down on her. Gail could see that not much was going to happen in the shower unless she helped Janet there too. "How about I wash you?"

Janet gave a weak nod.

Gail got undressed. Eyeing Janet's toned, supple body and mustering her self-control, Gail stepped into the shower. She lathered and rinsed Janet's silky blond tresses and then conditioned them. She reached for the soap and took a few fortifying breaths in preparation for having to run her hands all over Janet's beautiful body without going further. Pleased with herself that she had managed to keep her hands under control, Gail rinsed Janet and herself off. She turned off the water and led Janet out of the shower.

"Feel any better?" Gail asked as she toweled off Janet and then herself.

Janet nodded. "A little." Janet wrapped her damp hair in a towel.

"Good." Gail led her over to the bed and pulled back the covers. Once Janet was in bed, Gail padded around to the other side and got in with her.

Janet curled up in Gail's arms and closed her eyes.

Gail woke as daylight began to peek through the window blinds.

Next to her, Janet stirred and then stretched, waking also. "What is..." Janet brought a hand to her head, apparently surprised that her hair was wrapped in a towel.

Gail chuckled. "Sleep well?"

"It would seem so." Janet gave Gail a sheepish smile as she removed the towel from her hair. Janet combed her fingers through her hair and shook it out.

"You look adorable," Gail said at the sight of Janet's tousled blond locks and sheepish smile.

Janet smiled. "Thanks." She gave Gail a light kiss. "And thank you for last night."

"Of course," Gail said, slipping an arm around Janet's shoulders.

"I know I was a bit of a wreck." Janet snuggled her head on Gail's shoulder.

"It's okay." Gail turned and planted a kiss on Janet's forehead then settled back on her pillow. "You could still do it, you know."

"Do what?" Janet asked.

"Start a business," Gail said.

Janet's brow wrinkled. "How?"

"What if you didn't have a bakeshop? What if you did something smaller?"

"What do you mean?"

"You can still start a business to make products and sell them. You can just find a commercial kitchen and rent time there instead of having to buy and equip your own place. It has a few drawbacks, I know…"

"No, you're right," Janet said. "If I did something like that, I probably wouldn't need a grant." She sat up, arranging her pillow against the headboard. Gail did the same and pulled the blanket up higher to cover them.

"Or, sometimes people start in their own kitchen," Gail continued, warming to her idea. "I don't know how it was in Connecticut, but in California, baked goods can be made in a home kitchen and then sold."

"If I could start in my own kitchen, it might be really easy," Janet said with growing enthusiasm.

"I think that there's some kind of brief course to take if you want to use a home kitchen. You should talk to Maria. She found out a lot when she looked into value-added products for the farm."

"I think I will," Janet said. "Who needs a grant? I can do this on my own!" She smiled broadly, then grabbed either side of Gail's face and gave her a silly kiss with a loud *mmwwaa* sound.

Gail laughed. "I'm glad you're feeling better."

"I am feeling better," Janet said. "You have much better ideas than Natalie. She only said I should try to get a different grant."

Natalie? Gail's smile fell. "You told Natalie?"

"Yeah, when I saw her last night for my dance lesson," Janet said with a slight frown. "But I don't think there are any other grants right now."

"Why did you tell Natalie before me?"

Janet frowned again. "I saw Natalie before I saw you yesterday. I just…told her." She shrugged.

Gail turned away. She wanted to shout: *But I'm your girlfriend, not Natalie! Why didn't you tell me first?* Instead, she sat silently, gnawing the inside of her cheek. Why was Natalie important enough for Janet to tell first? Was Janet becoming that close to Natalie? Janet and Natalie did spend an awful lot of time together during those private classes each week. Was something going on between them?

Janet took Gail's hand uncertainly and was dismayed when Gail only returned her handclasp loosely. Gail had become awfully quiet, gnawing the inside of her cheek. Did Gail have something against Natalie? Or was it just that her feelings were hurt by not being the first person Janet told about not getting the grant?

"I only found out about not getting the grant my last night in Las Vegas. I wanted to tell you that same night, but I was embarrassed. I decided to wait a day and tell you when I got back."

Gail grunted a response and moved her hand away.

"Gail?" Janet asked.

Gail looked over at Janet. "Did Natalie comfort you too?"

Janet squinted at Gail and drew back. She didn't like the tone in Gail's voice. "Yes, of course she comforted me. Like I said, she said I should try to get another grant. She gave me a hug."

"A hug? She hugs you? What else does she do?"

Janet stared. "What's that supposed to mean?"

"You see her every week, you tell her important things before you tell me, she hugs you. Just what kind of dance lessons is this Natalie giving?"

Janet tossed aside the covers and got out of bed. "What are you saying? You're asking if Natalie and I are, what? Fucking?" Janet grabbed the blanket, covering her nude body and leaving Gail with the sheet. "Is that what you think? Is that what these questions are about? How can you think that?" Janet gestured wildly with her arm that wasn't clutching the blanket to herself and glared at Gail. "Are you going to think that of all of my friends?"

"No...I...You see her every week... You tell her things..." Gail stammered.

"Yes, I see her every week because she's my dance instructor! I tell her things because she's a friend!" Janet let out an exasperated breath. She gathered her clothes and boots, went into the bathroom, and shut the door. She came of the bathroom, fully dressed.

Gail began scrambling out of bed. "Janet, I'm sorry. I didn't—"

Janet held up a hand to forestall her. She was too angry to listen right now. "I'm going home."

CHAPTER FOURTEEN

Gail quit trying to scramble out of bed and stayed where she was, seated on the edge of the bed, watching helplessly as Janet left the room. She wished she could take back her question. She had instantly known the answer from the hurt in Janet's eyes.

But Gail couldn't very well not ask Janet something about what was going on at the dance studio. Janet had known about the grant a whole day ago and couldn't be bothered to call? And instead had told Natalie the moment she saw her and then fallen into her arms for a hug? But Gail hadn't meant to imply that she thought they were fucking. It had only sounded like Natalie might be trying to put the moves on Janet with her hugs and whatever else. Were there kisses of supposed comfort too? Caresses?

Gail heard the front door close loudly, heard Janet's car start. The sound of the car's motor faded into the distance. The reality of Janet leaving sunk in, and Gail sat there, too shaken to move. This was the last way she thought the morning would go, considering that it had started with Janet naked in her bed. How had things changed so quickly? *Oh, yeah, when I basically accused my girlfriend of cheating.* Gail shook her head, disgusted with herself. She was pretty sure she was falling in love with Janet and now she had driven her from her house with a stupid question. She stared down at her hands in her lap. There was a hollow feeling in her stomach. She had really messed things up, and she wasn't sure how badly. What if Janet didn't forgive her?

On the elliptical trainer at the gym, Janet pumped her arms and legs furiously. Did Gail really think she had something on the side with Natalie? How could Gail think such a thing about her? Just when the morning felt so perfect. Just when Janet thought she was falling in love. Did Gail really think Janet would hurt her like that? Especially after she had made it clear to Gail that she believed in monogamy? And especially since she knew that Gail had been hurt by a cheating ex?

Janet swiped at her perspiring face with a towel and kept pumping the steps and handles. She wished she had somebody to talk to about everything. She still felt kind of alone out here in California. Her friend Katie was all the way over in Connecticut. Janet knew Debbie, the bartender at the Danforth Bistro, but Debbie wasn't someone Janet got together to chat with outside of the restaurant. She considered Tina and Susan her friends now, but they were more Gail's friends than hers. There was Natalie, but she was out of the question for this particular problem. Janet thought of Katie again. She and Katie hadn't chatted in a few months. She resolved to call her when she got back to the apartment, or at least as soon as she turned on her phone again that had kept buzzing with Gail's calls.

Feeling marginally better after her workout, a shower, and a meal, Janet settled onto her couch to call Katie. With the three-hour time difference, Janet thought that now should be a good time to reach her.

"Janet! Hi!" Katie answered.

"Hi, Katie!" Happiness filled Janet at the joyful welcome in her friend's voice. But she wished she weren't so far away, wished that they could talk in person.

"How *are* you?" Katie asked warmly.

"Oh, pretty good."

There was a pause on Katie's end of the line. "There wasn't much enthusiasm in that 'pretty good.' How are things really?"

Katie knew her too well. "I'm okay…just some girlfriend trouble."

"You're seeing someone? That's great!"

"Yeah, it has been. I like her a lot."

"Then what's wrong?"

Janet brought Katie up to speed on everything that had gone on over the past few months, ending with her argument with Gail this morning.

"I hate to tell you," Katie said, "but if I were in Gail's place, my feelings would have been hurt too. I would have wanted to be the first person you told when you learned about not getting the grant."

"I wanted to tell Gail first. She was the first person I thought of to tell. If I hadn't been in another state because of my job, I would have been able to drive over to her house or invite her to my apartment and tell her all about not getting the grant."

"Yeah, but since you waited and since you're dancing each week with this other woman who is also a lesbian and you told her news like that first, I might start to wonder, too—however innocent the situation might be."

Janet took this in. Katie had never been afraid to tell it like it is. "I guess I can see how this might look to Gail."

"Yeah."

"Maybe I was too abrupt with her, but it hurts not to be trusted. I've given her no reason not to trust me. It's one thing for her to be upset that I didn't tell her first and another thing entirely for her to accuse me of having something with Natalie."

Katie didn't disagree.

"Thanks for letting me talk this through. You're always such a good listener."

"Any time."

"I want to hear about you. You must be due any week now."

"Yes, I'm pretty large. I'm due next month."

Gail sighed. Each of her calls to Janet had gone to voice mail. She hadn't expected otherwise, not after ruining a perfectly good morning. She just hoped she hadn't ruined things entirely. She realized she had probably sounded about as mature as a grade-schooler, asking jealously who had been told what first. And she realized how ridiculous she must have sounded jumping to conclusions that the hug had been anything more than friendly.

Gail recalled Susan's advice from a few months ago to stop worrying that relationships are going to end badly. She reminded herself to follow that advice. If she didn't, she was going to drive herself crazy or drive Janet away, or both.

Gail tried Janet's cell phone again even though she didn't really expect an answer this time either.

"Hello?"

Gail's heart leapt at the sound of Janet's voice. "Janet! It's me. I'm so sorry for what I said. Did you get my messages? Can you forgive me?"

"No," Janet said. "And yes."

No? Yes? Gail was fully prepared to grovel…

"No," Janet continued, "I only just turned my phone on again. I don't think I need to listen to the messages now. And—"

"—You're right. I can apologize to you right this very minute while I have you on the line and you won't have to listen to a bunch of voice mails."

"…And yes, I forgive you."

Gail wasn't sure she had heard correctly. "…You forgive me?"

"Yes."

Gail sagged with the relief of knowing that she hadn't wrecked things with Janet.

"What you asked me was really hurtful, but I can see how things might have seemed to you when I told Natalie something that important to me before telling you."

"The last thing I want to do is hurt you. I'm so sorry."

"I believe you, Gail. I'm sorry, too, but either you trust me or you don't."

"I *do* trust you. In my heart, I knew the answer before I asked the question about Natalie. I can't tell you how sorry I am to have made you think otherwise."

That afternoon, Janet's phone buzzed with a text message from Gail. *Come boating with me tomorrow?*

Boating? Janet texted back.

Yes, on the Delta.

It took Janet only a moment to decide. *Sounds fun.*

Come over at 10.

Okay.

CHAPTER FIFTEEN

When Janet pulled into Gail's driveway on Saturday morning, Gail came out to greet her, Bo not far behind. Gail gave her a smile that looked hesitant. Did she doubt that Janet had really forgiven her? Janet herself had some lingering hurt, but Janet didn't want there to be doubts between them. She smiled at Gail, approached, and then pulled her in for a kiss that she hoped would make her feelings clear.

Gail wrapped her arms around her, responding in kind.

"Good morning," Janet said, breaking the kiss.

"Mmm, good morning," Gail said, smiling broadly now.

Bo squirmed for attention. Janet bent down to pet him, and Gail joined in.

Gail straightened and brushed her hands. "All right, Bo, that's enough. I want to show Janet my boat." Gail put her arm around Janet and gestured to the motorboat resting on a trailer hitched to her truck. "Take a look."

"That's your boat? Wow! I just figured you had borrowed or rented a boat. You're full of surprises, Ms. Lawrence!"

Gail grinned.

"Let me see it up close."

"Sure thing." Gail offered Janet her arm, and Janet hooked her own arm through as they walked over to the boat. Janet stopped and ran her hands over the speedboat's shiny surface. The boat was about sixteen feet in length with two main seats and a bench seat that looked like it could hold three other people. It was a cream color with a jaunty blue stripe running around the rim.

"I guess my boat is a bit of a luxury," Gail said as she looked on, "but I don't go out of town on vacation very often because there is so much to do at the farm all the time, and the boat lets me take some fun day trips. Bo loves to come along and play in the water. What do you think of it?"

"I think it looks like it must be a lot of fun!"

"Yeah, it is. It's not a racing boat, but it's fast. And it's big enough to be comfortable, but small enough to get through most of the channel gates on the Delta."

Janet nodded. The seats did look comfortable. And everything was very clean. Gail obviously took good care of her boat. Janet appreciated that Gail was sharing it with her. "You know what else I like about it?" Janet asked with a smile.

"What?" Gail asked.

"That it will easily hold the ice chest I brought; I wasn't sure what you had in mind for lunch, but I thought we could picnic."

"A picnic? That will be great!"

Gail pulled into one of the state recreation areas south of Danforth on the Sacramento River. Good weather had drawn the crowds to the park, and Gail maneuvered around other vehicles to get her truck and trailer to a spot at the top of the steep boat launch ramp. She turned to Janet. "Okay, this is the place. I just need to get the boat unhooked from the trailer and into the water."

"Do you need any help?" Janet asked.

"Think you can keep a hold of Bo while I launch the boat? Sometimes he gets too wild and starts splashing in the water while I'm still in the middle of things."

Janet turned to Bo, who was seated behind them. "Bo, do you do that?"

Bo whined excitedly.

Janet laughed and turned to Gail. "I see you gave me the tough chore, but I think I can manage it."

Gail chuckled and got out of the truck, leaving Janet to unfasten Bo's seat belt tether and harness, and attach his leash. Janet was so good with Bo. Maybe Bo would mind her nicely and not cause chaos at the launch ramp. Gail began unhooking the cables securing the boat to the trailer. She finished with the last one and came back around to find Bo patiently sitting at Janet's side where she stood by the truck.

Gail shook her head. "Bo, I think you might have met your match."

Janet smiled and gave Bo a pat.

Gail thought she might have met her match in Janet, too, and wanted to tell her so—wanted to tell Janet that she was falling in love. But she wasn't sure Janet would be ready to hear it so soon after the accusations Gail had thrown at her yesterday. Gail was amazed that Janet had agreed to come boating at all after the things Gail had said, and Gail intended to make today a special day to help make up for her behavior.

"Okay, let me get the boat in the water." Gail got into her truck and backed the trailer down the ramp until the rear of her boat was well into the water, with the trailer wheels completely submerged. She got out, walked onto the small floating dock alongside the boat ramp, and hopped into the boat. She started the engine and slowly backed the boat off the trailer and into the water. Quickly looping rope around a cleat, she tied the boat to the dock, stepped onto the dock, and briskly walked back to Janet and Bo.

"Very impressive work," Janet said.

"Thank you, ma'am." Gail had tried extra hard to look smooth in front of Janet. She gave her a little salute and smiled. "Give me a sec to park the truck, and I'll be right back." She drove the truck to the parking area, then walked back once more to Janet and Bo. "Are you ready to go boating?"

Janet nodded, smiling, and Bo barked excitedly.

"Then let's go!" Gail led them down the dock, helped Janet and Bo into the boat, and then got in herself. When everyone was suited up with a life vest, Bo included, Gail undid the rope tethering her boat to the dock, started the engine, and idled them through the no-wake zone.

Bo rested his front paws on the transom and peered eagerly at all the sights around them.

"Don't you look handsome in that orange vest, Bo," Janet said from her seat next to Gail.

Bo was too excited to pay much attention to compliments, but Gail looked over at her.

"Handsome goes double for you, sailor," Janet said, her gaze drifting over Gail's body.

Gail smiled. "Thanks." Gail had worn this tank top just for Janet, knowing that it showed off her toned shoulders and arms. Under Janet's continued gaze, she felt her nipples tighten. When her life vest brushed against them, they tightened even more. She reached to adjust the vest to ease the friction.

Janet was smirking now. "Maybe I can help you with those later."

"What? How did you…"

Janet gave her a smile. "I know how responsive certain areas of you are."

A grin spread across Gail's face. "Is that so?"

"Uh-huh." Janet licked her lips.

Gail adjusted her vest again and swallowed. "Have a little mercy on a poor woman trying to drive a boat. But your offer of help sounds wonderful." Gail wanted very much for Janet to come back into her bed so that Gail could make things right after yesterday morning's abrupt end. She longed to feel Janet's caresses, her body against her own. Gail's groin responded to the idea. She looked over at Janet again. "Maybe you can help with another area too?"

"Yes, I'm sure I can be of assistance there, as well," Janet said with another smile.

"I definitely look forward to your, uh, assistance."

Gail passed a posting that delineated the end of the no-wake zone, so she increased the throttle. As the bow of the boat rose, Janet leaned back in her seat, a grin appearing on her face. Gail liked seeing it. She adjusted the controls, settling the boat into a smooth ride on top of the water. "Doing okay?" Gail asked.

"Yeah, this is fun! I see why you like it. And it's pretty out here too."

Gail nodded. Trees and tall grasses lined the broad river. Some areas allowed glimpses of the surrounding farmland. The water sparkled from the reflected sunlight.

"Quick—look over there by the bank!" Gail pointed at the sleek brown body gliding through the water. "See the otter?"

"Otter?" Janet followed her pointing finger. "Oh yeah! I see it! What a cute little thing!"

"It probably has a den nearby."

"That's so neat! Maybe we'll see more."

"Maybe. There are a lot of birds here too. This area is popular with birdwatchers."

Gail continued to navigate the waters of the river, enjoying the sunshine on her skin, the breeze in her hair, and Janet by her side. She steered the boat around a bend, and the beach and picnic area where she planned to take Janet came into view. The wide swath of shore was full of people, either relaxing on beach towels, playing in the sand, or wading and splashing in the water.

"Oh, what a pretty beach! And at the river too!" Janet said.

Gail smiled. "Yeah, I thought we'd stop here. Not only is it pretty, but it's also one of the beaches that allows dogs." She reached back to pat Bo.

"Sounds perfect." Janet smiled.

Gail maneuvered the boat to a mooring along the riverbank off to the side of the beach. She tied the boat off and helped Janet and Bo ashore. Bo was straining at his leash. "Let's take Bo down to the beach to let him play, and then we'll come back for the ice chest when we want to eat."

They joined the other beachgoers. Gail released Bo from his leash, and he sprinted for the water, jumping and splashing once he reached it. Gail took out a ball that she had brought and threw it for him.

Bo retrieved the ball and ran up with it, dropping it at Janet's feet. He looked up expectantly, tongue lolling. Janet laughed, picked the ball up, and threw it for him.

"Have I told you that you look lovely today?" Gail asked. Janet's blond hair had a golden luster in the afternoon sunlight, her skin had a beautiful light summer tan, and her blue eyes were bright and lively.

Janet smiled. "Thank you." She looked askance at the crowded beach and picnic area. "Is it okay to give you a kiss you out here?"

Gail followed Janet's gaze. "Sure. You think our fellow beachgoers might mind?"

Janet shrugged. "I know California is fairly tolerant, but there is still plenty of homophobia to go around."

"True. But I think we're among a docile crowd here. Besides, Bo and I would protect you if need be."

"Oh Gail, now I really want to kiss you." Janet reached for Gail and gave her a firm, lingering kiss that Gail thoroughly enjoyed. Gail hadn't said what she'd said just to get a kiss, though. She'd meant that she would protect Janet. But it didn't look like it would be necessary today at least, because none of the beachgoers were paying them any attention.

Bo continued to bound up with the ball, and they played several more rounds of fetch with him. "I think we might finally be wearing him down," Gail said.

"That's good, because I see one of the picnic tables becoming available. Do you want to see if we can get it?"

Gail followed her gaze to where a group of people was tidying the remains of their lunch at a nice partially shaded table in the covered, open-sided pavilion. "Yes, let's. I need to go get the ice chest from the boat, though." Gail attached Bo's leash.

"I'll take Bo and grab the table," Janet said, reaching for Bo's leash.

"Okay." Gail passed the leash to Janet and then got the ice chest and a satchel with food and water for Bo from the boat.

Gail set the ice chest on the picnic table at the end where Janet was sitting. Bo was on the ground beside her. Gail got Bo's portable dishes out of the satchel and filled them for him while Janet took their lunch out of the ice chest. Gail had never brought anyone here before, let alone had a picnic here before, but everything felt so natural and easy with Janet.

"This lunch looks wonderful," Gail said. Janet had set a meal of sandwiches, potato salad, grapes, and bottled iced tea on the table.

"I'm glad." Janet smiled. "Thanks for this day, Gail. I'm having a fantastic time."

They ate while they watched boaters and kayakers pass by on the river. Janet grew a little quiet over the course of the meal, and Gail was starting to get a hollow feeling in the pit of her stomach that Janet's mind might be on yesterday's events.

Janet fidgeted with her empty bottle of iced tea on the table. "My last dance lesson is next week."

"Oh?" Gail asked cautiously.

"Yes, Natalie's group class is finishing up that week and she's taking some time for vacation before her college semester starts." Janet looked at Gail. "But, that doesn't mean that I won't see Natalie anymore. She's a friend now."

"I know," Gail said. "I wouldn't ask that. I was only hurt and handling it badly."

"I'm sorry you weren't the first person I told. I know that you were waiting almost as anxiously to hear if I won the grant as I was. I just didn't want you to think I was a loser."

"A loser? You're not a loser." Gail took Janet's hands in hers.

"I felt like one. But I don't feel like one anymore, not after the ideas you gave me about how I could start a business without the grant."

"Good. I know you'll be successful. And I'm done worrying too. I trust you. I think I always have."

Janet gave Gail's hands a squeeze. "Good, because I don't think we can have much of a relationship without trust. I trust you too."

Gail squeezed back. "I'm sorry I didn't realize my trust soon enough not to ask you that stupid question yesterday."

"It's okay, Gail. Let's forget about it. I know that your ex hurt you."

"Yeah, let's forget about her too. I want to finish enjoying the rest of the day with you. Are you ready to get back on the water?"

Janet nodded. They repacked the ice chest and Bo's gear and walked back to the boat with Bo.

Gail hopped into the boat and stowed their gear and then helped Janet and Bo aboard. When Janet and Bo were situated, she untied the boat and guided them back out on the river. After she had reached a broad section of water, Gail turned to Janet and gestured at the wheel. "Would you like to try it?"

"Um…"

Gail smiled. "No worries for either of us, remember? I'll help you while you try the wheel."

"Okay," Janet said, smiling back.

Gail idled the boat and got up from her seat. "Here, take the driver's seat and I'll show you how to work the throttle so that you'll be able to control the engine speed when you drive."

Janet's eyes were wide, but she gamely got into the driver's seat. Gail stood in the space behind her and demonstrated the boat's controls. "Ready to try it yourself?"

"Yes, but I think I would feel better standing up at first like you were doing earlier. It's kind of hard to see over the front of the boat when it rises out of the water as we go faster."

"That's fine. And you'll get used to that as you drive."

Janet stood. "Okay, but stay close."

"Not a problem." Gail moved closer to her and rested her hands on Janet's waist below her life vest. She kissed the back of her neck and slid her arms the rest of the way around her waist. She rested her chin on her shoulder and turned to kiss her cheek.

"When I said 'stay close,' I didn't realize it would be so distracting," Janet said with a smile.

Gail laughed, kissed her cheek once more, and then released her. "I'll behave."

Janet slowly increased the throttle, her smile broadening as the boat picked up speed.

"Good," Gail said as they reached a comfortable speed. She had widened her stance and was holding onto the back of the chair for stability to stay near Janet while she learned to drive. "Just remember to use small movements while you steer, because the boat is really responsive."

Janet moved the wheel a little to one side experimentally. "It is!" Janet turned the wheel the other way, moving the boat in a gradual wide arc. "This is fun!"

"You're doing great."

"Is Bo okay back there?" Janet asked.

Gail glanced at Bo, who was grinning his doggy grin as he panted happily. "Oh yeah, he loves it."

Janet steered some more big zigzags, smiling all the while. As a speedboat towing a water skier and leaving a choppy wake appeared in the distance, Janet eased the throttle. "I think you'd better take over."

"Sure, but that was some nice driving." Gail took the wheel, remained standing, and Janet sat down in the passenger seat. Gail resumed speed and steered them over the waves left by the other boat, trying to minimize the bounce for Janet.

"You're so sexy, Gail."

Gail warmed at the sudden compliment. She turned to Janet and grinned. "Thanks."

"You look so confident standing there. The way you've been commanding this boat all day is such a turn-on. I can't wait to get my hands on you later." Janet's eyes were practically devouring her, and Gail loved it.

"Then I had better get us back home," Gail said, increasing the throttle.

Gail pulled her truck and trailer into her driveway. As eager as she was to get into her house with Janet, Gail hoped that Janet's mood wouldn't be wrecked upon entering her bedroom, the scene of their argument from yesterday. Gail had changed the sheets and comforter on her bed, dusted the furniture, and vacuumed the carpet in an attempt to erase all traces of her hurtful words of the past. She hoped it would help. Even though

Gail felt their argument was settled after their conversations about it, it was still a fresh memory.

Janet turned to her with a wrinkled brow. "Is everything all right?"

Gail took a breath. "Just a little nervous about going inside, I guess." She faced Janet. "I tidied up the bedroom for us."

"Hmm. That was thoughtful of you." Janet laid her palm softly along Gail's cheek. "But no worries about that argument anymore for either of us, remember?" She leaned in and gave Gail a kiss.

Gail smiled. "Okay."

Janet fixed her with a steady gaze. "Now, I seem to remember offering some 'help and assistance' in two important areas of your body earlier today, and I don't want to wait any longer."

Gail grinned. "You don't have to tell me twice." She opened her door and got out. Once she had undone Bo from his seat belt tether and harness, she let him out into the yard and led Janet into the house and into the bedroom.

She watched Janet take in the fresh bedding.

Janet turned to her with a smile. "I do like what you've done with the place." She moved closer to Gail and put her hands on her shoulders. "Have I also mentioned how much I like how you look in a tank top?" She caressed Gail's shoulders and arms and then smoothed her hands down Gail's chest, stopping just shy of her breasts as she backed her toward the bed.

"Um…" Gail's pulse pounded and her nipples tightened.

"I haven't stopped thinking about your breasts all day. The way they fill out this tank top has been driving me crazy." Janet lowered her hands and brushed Gail's now protruding nipples with her thumbs.

Gail's breath caught.

"I haven't stopped thinking about how much I want to touch them." Janet lifted Gail's tank top over her head and tossed it aside. She continued to thumb her nipples through her bra, and Gail felt them harden even more.

Janet removed Gail's bra and tossed it aside too. She thumbed the nipples again, this time skin on skin. She gave them a slight squeeze. Gail groaned. "Oh…that feels so good."

"And most of all, I haven't stopped thinking about how I want to run my tongue all around them." Janet bent to lick from the bottom edge of one breast to its hard nipple, taking the firm bud of flesh into her mouth and manipulating it with her tongue.

"Janet…" Gail slid her arms around Janet's shoulders.

Janet moved to the other nipple and closed her lips over it, eliciting another groan from Gail. She reached to undo Gail's shorts.

Gail hastily helped her push them off, along with her underwear, and then hurried to remove Janet's clothes as well.

Janet paused to admire Gail's nude body, but Gail couldn't wait any longer. Gail stepped forward and captured Janet's mouth in a searing kiss. She slid a hand to the back of Janet's neck and continued to kiss her deeply, wrapping her other arm around her and pulling their bodies together. She felt Janet's swollen wetness press against her thigh, and it made her groin throb. She held Janet and backed onto the bed with her, positioning a leg between Janet's legs. Gail cupped the flesh of Janet's buns, pressing Janet's hot center and engorged clitoris firmly against her thigh.

Janet moaned at the pressure and began to move her hips.

"Oh, yeah," Gail said. "Janet…Janet you turn me on so much." Gail thrust her own hips, seeking.

Janet reached a hand to Gail's aroused clitoris. She ran her fingers along its slickened length, once, twice, again. Gail's breathing became more ragged with Janet's every stroke.

Janet increased her pace against Gail's thigh. "I'm going to come soon," she said breathlessly.

"Me too," Gail rasped. Her clit began to quiver.

Janet cried out in climax, bringing Gail with her as she gave her clit one last stroke, and Gail rode out the orgasm with her.

"Gail?" Janet said softly.

"Yes?"

"I love you."

"I love you too."

CHAPTER SIXTEEN

Janet drove through the streets of downtown Seattle on a return visit to Centennial Hospital. Despite the rental car agency giving her the same giant sport utility vehicle as before and despite the weather being gray as before, Janet's mood was good. She had a strong, sensitive, and sexy girlfriend whom she loved and who loved her. She just hoped that Gail could keep putting up with her business travel. Janet knew it couldn't be easy. Janet could barely put up with it herself, and that was before she had met Gail.

That grant would have made trying a different career path a lot easier, but as she had said to Gail, she no longer regretted not winning. Maybe not getting the grant was for the best. The home kitchen idea was what intrigued her now. Maybe it would be smartest to begin her business on a small scale since there was so much to learn. She didn't really need a bakeshop to sell candied nuts or cookies when she already had a kitchen. She could grow her business at her own pace.

The first thing she would do when she got a chance this week was talk to Maria for information about value-added products.

Having a plan to embark on something that gave Janet more satisfaction and more control over her job and life was going to make the next few days here in Seattle during the hospital's accreditation survey a lot less draining.

Gail sat down in her favorite recliner with a stack of seed catalogs and a pen. She needed to decide what seeds to buy to plant for her fall crops for her CSA customers. And she wanted to choose a few items especially for Janet. Gail was so glad their relationship was back on track, and it thrilled her to be planning her future with Janet in mind, even if it was something as simple as choosing what vegetables that they might like to have in the fall. It would also give her something to do at least one evening while Janet was out of town.

She opened the first catalog and circled her choices for carrots, lettuces, and radishes, ordering several varieties of each. Next, she carefully perused the beets. Janet made such excellent salads with her beets. Janet might enjoy cooking with a few other varieties of beets, as well. Gail circled five varieties. Speaking of salads, she needed to order more arugula seeds and spinach seeds.

Gail hoped things were going well in Seattle. She knew that Janet had gone to help the pharmacy department through an important survey, and she didn't doubt that Janet would be well prepared, but it seemed like it would be just another pressure-filled trip that Janet wouldn't get to enjoy. It made Gail recall her own days as a financial analyst back in Los Angeles. She didn't miss that at all. Even if farming came with its own set of stresses, it was at least a job she liked.

She reached for the next catalog. Was this where she had gotten that tasty heirloom cauliflower? She wanted Janet to be able to try it. She ordered it and a couple of other varieties. Too bad about that grant. What would Janet decide now about starting a business? There was a lot of competition in baked goods, but Gail knew Janet well enough to know that if she put her mind to something she would succeed. Gail circled broccoli and a few varieties of leeks. Maybe she should take Janet out when she got back into town from her hard week in Seattle, just somewhere casual and relaxing, like the Danforth Bistro, as she knew Janet would be tired. Despite the changes in the food there, it was still a restaurant they both liked since it was the place where Janet had first seen Gail.

* * *

On Thursday, Janet sat in the Seattle airport, waiting for her flight home. Maybe now would be a good time to reach Maria.

Even as she took out her phone, it buzzed in her hand with a call from Aaron. Why did he always call the day after a hospital survey when he knew she would be sending him a report full of the very details he wanted to know? She took a breath and picked up.

"How did the survey go?" he asked.

"Really well. The surveyors hardly docked the pharmacy department any points at all."

"Uh-huh, uh-huh," Aaron said.

Janet could tell that he'd stopped listening after he heard that things went well. He was probably on his computer.

He cleared his throat. "Just a little heads-up—I had Elaine send out the final itinerary for next week's meetings in Boston. You're flying on Sunday now."

"The weekend? Why?" That was time Janet spent with Gail, not with Rockland Healthcare Solutions.

"There were some scheduling issues later in the week with some of the managers, so we had to move up some of the meetings to Monday."

Janet was silent as she absorbed this.

"Look on the bright side, you'll be nice and rested for the meetings since things went so well there in Seattle!"

Janet got off the phone before she said something she would regret. She pushed in the number for Maria at the farm office. Nothing like a little extra motivation from Aaron to embark on the journey of starting a brand-new career.

"Lawrence Farms, how may I help you?"

"Hi, Maria, it's Janet, Janet Webber…"

"Janet, yes, hello. Gail said you might call this week."

"She did? That was considerate of her." Janet smiled at the thought of Gail. "Do you have a moment to talk?"

"Certainly," Maria said pleasantly.

"Okay. I'm not sure how much Gail has told you, but I'm considering starting a home kitchen business."

"Yes, Gail told me that you applied for a grant but didn't get it. I'm sorry to hear that."

"Thank you, but I think things might actually be simpler for me without the grant. I was hoping that you could tell me more about home kitchens and anything else that you think that might help."

"I'd be glad to." Maria paused, as though gathering her thoughts. "It's true that products can be made in a home kitchen, but there are limitations. The main thing is that the products must be items that don't require refrigeration."

"That sounds okay," Janet said. "Cookies and candied nuts don't need refrigeration."

"Yes, and I remember those cookies. I know they would be popular with our customers. That reminds me—home kitchen sales can't exceed a certain dollar amount per year. I don't remember the exact number, but it would be easy to find out again."

"Hmm," Janet said. She should be so lucky that her sales got too high—then she could quit her regional management job for sure.

"If you're worried about that, you could rent time in a commercial kitchen. There is no sales limit with that, but when I looked into commercial kitchens, I couldn't find any nearby. The closest ones are at least an hour away."

"That would be a lot of driving if I need to go there and back every time I needed to bake something," Janet said.

"And the rental rates were high."

"Hmm," Janet said again. Commercial kitchens didn't sound ideal, but she wasn't against them as an option.

"Another important thing to know for either kind of kitchen is that there are permits required."

"Yes, I figured that," Janet said. "Is that through the health department?"

"Yes, their website has a list."

"A list, huh?" Janet asked.

Maria made a sympathetic noise.

But permits were no big deal; Janet was used to dealing with permits in pharmacies. "And Gail mentioned something about there being a course of some sort to take."

"Yes, I remember a food processor course on the list. When I clicked the link, it took me to courses with video modules that could be done online."

"That sounds convenient. Thanks so much for this, Maria."

"No problem. And good luck!" There was a pause. "I hope it works out, Janet. All of it."

Janet understood what she meant. "Thank you. Me too."

CHAPTER SEVENTEEN

Janet stepped to the music playing over the sound system in the dance studio, enjoying the challenge of the fast footwork and clapping of the Chattahoochee. The song ended, and Janet smiled at Natalie. "That was a fun one."

Natalie smiled back. "Yeah, I thought it would be a good dance to end your lessons." Natalie clicked off the sound system.

"It was. I'm so glad I took the lessons from you. It's been so much fun, and I feel a lot better on the dance floor now."

"Thanks, I've had fun teaching you. You've been a great student." Natalie handed Janet a dance sheet that listed the steps they had just practiced. "Just keep dancing, and you'll get even better."

"Don't worry, I'll still do my homework even though class is over." Janet scanned the sheet. As the level of the dances progressed, it wasn't so much that the moves became more difficult, it was that the dances became harder to memorize because they involved more steps. Janet collected her purse and slipped the dance sheet into it. She walked out of the studio with

Natalie, who turned out the lights and then locked the door behind them.

A sudden feeling of sadness enveloped Janet. These dance lessons with Natalie had been one of the bright spots in her workweek. Janet turned to Natalie. "I know you'll be busy with your coursework starting up soon, but maybe you and Ana could come dancing with Gail and I at The Pink Stallion sometime."

"Yeah, we should make plans sometime," Natalie said.

Janet nodded. She hoped Gail would be open to the idea. Janet liked to think that Gail was okay with Natalie now, but she wasn't certain. "Yes, we have each other's numbers, so let's be sure and stay in touch."

Janet hugged Natalie goodbye and headed for her car.

Gail waited impatiently at a railroad crossing for a long and slow-moving freight train. Showing up as a surprise at the studio to take Janet out after her last lesson wasn't going to be much of a surprise if she couldn't even get there. After a good ten minutes, the train finally passed, and the crossing guards lifted. Gail drove on.

She pulled into a parking space along the curb across the street from the studio. Janet's car was in the lot. Good—she hadn't left yet. Gail undid her seat belt and reached for the door handle, but stopped when she saw a young woman approach Janet's car. Who was that? Natalie? It had to be. The woman was dressed for line dancing with her boots and faded jeans, not to mention the tank top over her trim body.

Torn between wanting to go see Janet and wanting to know what was happening, Gail continued to watch. The woman bent down and tapped on the passenger window of Janet's car. Gail could discern movement through the car's windows, could make out Janet leaning over the console toward the window. A brief conversation took place. Then, the woman got in.

Gail was beginning to feel like some kind of stalker as she watched all of this from her truck. And Gail was not a stalker. She had only come here to take Janet out, but it looked like Natalie had beaten her to it. Or, at least that's what she hoped was going on. She debated going over to find out for certain what was going on. It occurred to Gail, though, that if she interrupted Janet and Natalie at this point, Janet might wonder what she was doing here so long after the lesson. Janet might think that Gail had started keeping tabs on her time with Natalie, that Gail still didn't trust her. And Gail wasn't going to let that happen.

Gail started her truck. She wasn't going to hang around like some kind of crazy jealous girlfriend to watch whatever happened next and she certainly wasn't going to follow them, even if the thought had briefly crossed her mind. She had told Janet that she trusted her, and she was going to do her best to do just that. She was going to believe that there was some innocent explanation for what she was seeing. Her heart couldn't take it if there wasn't. Gail pulled her truck away from the curb and headed home.

"My apartment building is coming up on the right." Natalie pointed to a large brown and white apartment complex in the next block. "You can just park at the curb."

Janet slowed and pulled into a parking space.

"Thank you so much for the ride. Do you have time to come in?" Natalie asked. "I want to introduce you to Ana. I've told her a lot about you, and I'm sure she would like to meet you. She likes to cook too."

"Sure, I'd love to meet her," Janet said. She turned the car off.

Natalie led Janet up a walkway to the door of one of the units. "Wait here a minute while I let Ana know that there's someone with me."

Janet nodded. As Natalie opened the door to let herself in, Janet caught an appealing aroma of food cooking, maybe something involving garlic and oil.

Natalie returned a moment later with a woman who also looked to be in her twenties and who had chocolate-colored eyes, light brown skin, long dark brown hair, and a cute, dimpled smile. "Janet, I'd like you to meet my girlfriend, Ana Olvera. Ana, this is Janet Webber."

Ana shook Janet's hand. "It's nice to meet you, Janet. Thanks so much for giving Natalie a ride tonight."

"No problem. I'm glad I could help. It wouldn't have been a good time to sit out there and wait for someone from roadside assistance to come give her car a jumpstart or to change out the battery."

"Not only that," Natalie said, "but I would have missed dinner, and Ana's cooking is too good to miss." She put her arm around her girlfriend and kissed her temple. "The car can wait until tomorrow."

Ana smiled and blushed. "Speaking of dinner, Janet, we'd like to invite you to stay and have dinner with us."

"Um…" Janet hesitated, not wanting to impose but curious as to what dish was the source of that appealing aroma.

Natalie opened the door wider. "Come on in. Ana cooked plenty. Do you like Mexican food?"

"Yes," Janet said, and stepped into the apartment.

* * *

Friday night, Gail and Janet sat at the bar in the Danforth Bistro with glasses of wine that Debbie had served them. They had been there a couple times together, and Debbie always seemed happy to see them again. Neither the bar nor the restaurant was very crowded.

"It feels good to sit here with you and relax," Janet said. She sipped her wine. "Things went well in Seattle, but it's been a long week."

Gail listened as Janet described her time in Seattle. Gail wanted to know more about Janet's previous night with Natalie but was doing her best not to seem impatient. She caught Janet up on her own workweek.

Debbie returned. "Ladies? Anything to eat?"

"I'm having the quarter chicken with shoestring fries until they resurrect my veggie burger," Janet said.

Debbie grinned. "Actually, I've heard some talk."

"You have?" asked Janet hopefully. She glanced at Gail.

"Yeah," Debbie said. "As you can see, business is a little slow. I've heard talk that they may do away with some of the changes and start ordering from local farms again."

"That would be great!"

Gail nodded. She was not surprised that the cost-cutting measures had cost the bistro business. She had told Robert that he was making a mistake canceling the contracts with local suppliers in favor of a regional distributor when she spoke with him that night in April. "Robert knows how to find me," she said. "In the meantime, I'll have the quarter chicken with shoestring fries too."

Janet was still smiling when Debbie left to enter their orders into the computer.

"You're dreaming of that veggie burger, aren't you?" Gail asked.

"Yes. The very thought of having that wonderful, savory patty with your walnuts again is making me salivate."

Gail laughed. "You're a little crazy." She gave Janet's thigh an affectionate squeeze.

"Maybe," Janet admitted, "but only a little." She bumped Gail's shoulder playfully. "Let me tell you about the delicious food I had last night!"

Gail turned toward her, smiling expectantly. She loved Janet's enthusiasm about food.

"Actually, let me start from the beginning," Janet said. "Natalie had a dead battery, so I gave her a ride to..." Janet stopped talking and cocked her head at Gail.

Janet must have seen realization dawn on Gail's face about what had happened last night. Gail felt herself redden now that she was going to have to explain herself. "I was there," Gail said.

"What do you mean?"

"Last night. I was across the street from the studio. I came to take you out after your last lesson. I wanted to surprise you."

"What? Why didn't you let me know you were there?"

"I was late. Because of a train. By the time I got there, Natalie was getting into the car with you. It would have seemed strange if all of a sudden I appeared and interrupted. So I left."

Janet frowned. "Gail, that's too bad. I would have loved to go out with you. If you were there, you should have said something."

"It's okay. I didn't want you to get the wrong idea."

Janet sat quietly, fiddling with her wineglass.

Gail's stomach started to fall. Janet must think the worst of her—that Gail had been keeping track of her and Natalie.

"You know, I thought I heard a truck that sounded like yours last night," Janet said.

Gail's stomach bottomed out. She braced herself for trouble.

"I'm proud of you," Janet said.

"What? You are?" Gail felt like she could breathe again.

Janet took Gail's hands. "Yes. You didn't freak out. I know it can't have been easy for you not to jump to conclusions after seeing Natalie get into my car after my dance lesson."

"It wasn't. But I knew I could trust you."

"I'm so glad, Gail."

Gail paused. "So you believe me that I wasn't checking up on you and Natalie or anything?"

"Yes. I know that you may have a little bit of trouble still, but I know you wouldn't lie to me or follow me around like that."

"Good. I wouldn't. Thanks for believing me. I love you."

"I love you too," Janet said. Janet leaned over and gave her a kiss.

Debbie came back with their dinners. Janet popped some fries in her mouth and then started in on her chicken.

"So, back to last night," Janet continued. "I gave Natalie a ride to her apartment. Her girlfriend had been cooking, and there were wonderful smells wafting out of the apartment. Fortunately, they asked me to stay for dinner."

"That was nice of them. What was it?"

"It was something called *picadillo*. Ana made it with ground beef, onions, garlic, tomatoes, olives, almonds, and raisins. It was so good. She served it with rice and salad. I ate such a big helping of it, I wasn't even hungry for breakfast this morning."

Gail grinned at Janet's enthusiastic retelling of dinner.

"I told Ana that I'd like to make the dish for you sometime, and she shared the recipe with me. I wonder if it would work with your walnuts."

"I don't know, but I would love to taste it either way," Gail said. "And I still want to take you out. Let's go dancing at The Pink Stallion on Sunday and show off some of your moves now that your lessons are over. We could go with Tina and Susan."

"I would love to go dancing," Janet said. She sighed. "But I can't Sunday. I've got to fly that day to make it to the East Coast in time for meetings at headquarters on Monday."

Gail tried not to let her dismay show.

"I appreciate that you put up with my crazy schedule, Gail. I know it's difficult."

"I just worry that they're working you too hard. Now they're making you fly on the weekend."

"I'm not happy about it either. In fact, I talked to my landlord today to ask if he would let me use my apartment as a home kitchen."

"You mean the cheapskate who makes you wait a week before he does repairs?"

"One and the same. I was doubtful, too, but he said yes."

"Really?"

"Yes. He seems very in favor of entrepreneurship. He said that one of the other tenants also has a home business. The tenant has a unit with a garage and uses the space to make wooden toys to sell online."

"That's good news."

"Yes. I think a home kitchen would be the best place for me to start. I talked to Maria yesterday, and a commercial kitchen sounds like something I would need only after my business gets bigger."

"She mentioned that you called. I'm glad she could help."

"She also told me about permits and other requirements, so that's what I'll have to work on next."

"It sounds like you've decided to go ahead and start a business, then?"

"I think so. I think I can do it."

"I think you can too."

"Thanks, Gail. It's hard not to doubt myself about taking the leap to start a business, so your belief in me means a lot. I'll have my work cut out for me doing this, but that's nothing new." Janet finished the last of her dinner and set down her utensils. "Would you give me a rain check to go dancing next Sunday?"

"I could be convinced," she said archly.

"I can be very convincing. Let's go to my apartment."

CHAPTER EIGHTEEN

Janet walked through the austere but attractive modern lobby of Rockland Healthcare Solutions. She checked in with the receptionist before heading to the conference room where the pharmacy management meetings were being held. She had been to headquarters only once before, for some of her training as a regional account manager.

Past the lobby, the interior of the building became less attractive, with the design emphasis more on functionality. Janet walked long hallways full of doorways that opened to sparsely decorated rooms in muted industrial colors. There were workers at cubicles, and this deep into the building, the rooms did not have any windows, only fluorescent lighting. Had Gail's desk job in the high-rise in downtown Los Angeles been like this? No wonder she'd returned to the farm.

Janet turned and entered the conference room. Some people were already there, but Janet did not necessarily know or recognize them. Like herself, they each worked within their own regions of the country and only met at meetings like this.

Janet knew that she should take the opportunity to mingle and network with other people in the company's pharmacy management hierarchy, but she was tired from her cross-country flight and instead headed over to get herself some coffee from a coffee urn on a table in the corner.

At the sound of Aaron's booming voice, Janet turned. He had just walked in and was already busy glad-handing people. She turned back to fixing her coffee. He was an okay boss, but Janet wasn't in the mood this morning for his outsized personality, which only became more pronounced at events like this. She took a sip of her coffee and then put a smile on her face when she saw that he had noticed her. He made his way over.

"Janet! Good to see you!" He gave her hand such a hearty shake that she almost spilled the coffee she was holding in the other. "How's the old jet lag treating you?" He laughed loudly.

Janet managed to get in a few words of greeting and conversation as his barrage of welcoming continued. She was relieved when he moved away to turn his effusiveness on someone else. She found a seat and reached into her purse for some ibuprofen for a developing headache.

Jet lag wasn't the only thing bothering Janet. It had been almost a year since she had been back to the East Coast. Now that she was here, she was stuck at these meetings in Boston when she wanted to get to Fulton, Connecticut. She had planned to drive down to Fulton at the end of the week, and now that she was here she was getting antsy. She wanted to see her realtor and check on her house, and she and Katie had planned a visit. And on top of all the things to do in Fulton, Janet was preoccupied with permits and other requirements for her home kitchen.

She flipped through her schedule to see if there was a day she could skip out on some meetings. Members of upper management were speaking this morning with a luncheon to follow. Afterward, there were afternoon sessions. Today was not the best day to skip. Tomorrow was training on the new product and service offerings for clients, and those would be helpful sessions. She looked over Wednesday. The day revolved around topics in which she already felt confident, and she wondered if

Aaron would let her play hooky if she said she wanted to see her former staff and colleagues at Fulton Hospital. She could be back for Thursday's sessions on regulatory updates and patient safety insights.

After the luncheon, Janet caught Aaron's attention. When she broached the subject of going to Fulton Hospital, he seemed pleased. "I was going to talk to you about that."

"You were?"

"Yes. We want you to cover Katie when she takes maternity leave."

"What?" *Me?*

"It's your old job. It would be easy."

"But…" Janet began. *Wouldn't that be three months? Wasn't that how long maternity leave was?*

"You know everyone there, and they know you," Aaron said.

"But…I don't live here anymore."

"We'd put you in a nice hotel, of course."

"You want me to stay three months?" She was still trying to comprehend.

"It's not that long. I'll have Elaine arrange it all." Janet only vaguely noticed when he patted her on the shoulder and excused himself.

"I can't just…" Janet said but stopped when she realized she was now standing by herself.

Janet searched the room. There he was, casually chatting with someone else after dumping this on her. A fury rose. Aaron or whoever had made the decision could find someone else to foist this off on. Katie had said corporate had been delaying finding coverage for her. Now Janet knew why. She needed to get out of here before she made a scene. She stalked from the room, down the maze of industrial hallways, through reception, and out to the parking lot to her rental car. They would just have to miss her the rest of the day and probably the rest of the week, too, because the way she felt now, she wasn't going back. She had had enough of the flying, the hotels, the schedule that changed at everyone's whim but her own, all of it.

Janet drove to her hotel, packed her things, and checked out. She got into her rental car. She wanted badly to drive herself to the airport and get on the first flight home, but she had things to do in Fulton. The sooner she could check on her house, the sooner she could fly home. The conversation with Aaron kept replaying in her head. She was furious that they would stick her with this. She really hoped that Katie hadn't suggested her for the job. She did not want it at all. Maybe she would just drive straight to Fulton Hospital and find out what was going on. No, it was two hours away. Katie would have gone home by then. Janet heaved a sigh. Talking to Gail might calm her. She got out her phone and pressed Gail's number, but got voice mail and left a message.

Janet didn't wait any longer. She drove to Fulton, fuming about her job the entire way, checked into a hotel, and fell into an exhausted sleep.

Gail checked her phone after she stepped off her tractor. Two missed calls, one of them from Janet. She listened to Janet's voice mail. *They want me to stay. Do you believe it? I'll tell you more later.*

Gail stood there, the words *They want me to stay* buzzing in her head. Rockland wanted Janet to stay there? On the East Coast? Was Janet not coming back? Gail's world tilted on its axis.

Gail loved Janet. Janet understood her. Janet cared about the same things she cared about. Janet accepted her, worries and all. Plus, Janet was one of the loveliest women Gail had ever met. The thought that Janet might move back across the country was devastating, and Gail felt sick and tense.

Gail listened to the message again, trying to discern more from it. Janet's voice was annoyed but also resigned. Was Janet really going to stay there? And what had they asked her to stay for? Gail remembered that Janet's house hadn't even sold yet. Janet could easily move back in. Maybe this was something to do with her old hospital. Would Janet stay on the East Coast if she had a job where she didn't have to fly each week? And her friend Katie was there.

Katie. Katie was pregnant and due soon. Maybe that's all that was going on. Maybe Rockland just needed Janet to stay and help in the pharmacy temporarily. Gail felt some of the tension in her body release. She had gotten herself worked up for no reason. She needed to get a hold of herself. She was being ridiculous to think that Janet would leave her when they loved each other so deeply. She pressed the number to return Janet's call, but Janet's phone went to voice mail. Gail left a message.

Janet awoke hungry. She hadn't had any dinner last night. The last thing she had eaten was the food at the corporate luncheon before she talked to Aaron. Ugh, Aaron. Aaron, who assumed that she would uproot herself and stay here for months on end and that it was no imposition. Unbelievable. Janet threw off the covers and got out of bed.

She felt more levelheaded after breakfast. It was still early, too early for either her realtor or Katie to be in their offices, but not too early to go check on her house. She got into her car and drove over.

When she saw the overgrown grass and untended bushes in her front yard, she wasn't pleased. Her realtor was supposed to be coordinating care of the yard. It looked like the water hadn't been run in some time, either, as there were dry spots here and there. Janet let herself into the house and walked around. It was strange to be here. It seemed like a lifetime ago that she had lived here, and she couldn't imagine returning to that lifetime when she had a new life in Danforth. A new life with Gail.

Janet looked in the backyard. Same problem with dry spots as the front. She got out her cell phone to take a picture. Her phone showed a voice mail from Gail. Janet listened. *Janet, Is everything all right? I don't understand what's happening there. Call me back when you can.* Janet frowned at the sound of stress in Gail's voice. She tried to think of the message she had left Gail yesterday, but with the agitated state she had been in she couldn't remember her exact words. She pressed Gail's number to call her back but got voice mail. The time difference wasn't making it easy to reach each other. Janet left a message.

Janet opened the camera app on her phone and took several pictures of both the backyard and front yard of her house. The unkempt yards alone would be enough to deter many buyers, but Janet was beginning to wonder if her realtor was putting in the effort to even show the home at all. Time to go have a chat with him and see about canceling her contract.

The realtor was surprised to see her and obviously knew that he had dropped the ball. Even so, Janet had to raise a stink about the violation of her listing agreement to get out of her contract. Afterward, she went directly to another real estate office and listed her house with them, keeping her fingers crossed that they would do a better job. It was a nice house, after all, and shouldn't be difficult to sell. She stopped for something to eat before going to Fulton Hospital.

Gail sighed when she saw that she had missed another call from Janet. She pressed play and listened to the voice mail. *Gail, I meant to call you last night but I fell asleep. My boss made me so angry that I left Boston and drove to Fulton. I'm here taking care of some things. I'm at my house right now. There's so much to tell you. I'll try you again later. 'Bye.*

Gail took a breath. This message was just as confusing as the first. She thought she might go crazy if she didn't find out what was happening. She pressed Janet's number. Voice mail again. She hung up.

Janet walked through the door to the pharmacy administrative offices. Just as it had felt strange to be at her old house, it felt strange to be here. This wasn't her life anymore. She had new goals, new hopes and dreams. Dreams of a home kitchen, dreams of being her own boss, dreams of a future with Gail.

The secretary's desk was vacant; the secretary was probably at lunch. Just as well, because Janet didn't particularly want to reminisce about old times that she didn't particularly enjoy.

Janet walked over to Katie's office and stopped in the doorway. The sight of her friend made her smile. Katie was one part of her life here that she did miss. "Knock, knock!" Janet announced herself.

Katie looked up. "Janet! You're here early!" Katie made to push herself out of her chair to greet her friend.

"Whoa, that's okay," Janet protested as the very pregnant Katie attempted to stand up.

"Don't worry—the obstetrics wing isn't far," Katie said.

Janet let out a laugh and went to hug her friend. "It's so good to see you!"

"You too," Katie said. She hugged Janet and then released her. "But I thought you were going to be at the meetings at headquarters today."

Janet let out a sigh. "So did I, but I had to get out of there." She sat down in one of the chairs.

"What happened?" Katie asked. She sat down too, and listened as Janet explained.

"And then I left," Janet finished recounting her tale. "My absence has probably been noticed by now, but that's okay. I need a different job. I've realized it for a while."

"Yeah," Katie said.

"That's why starting my own business appeals to me so much." Janet updated Katie on her business plans since not getting the grant.

"Wow! It sounds like you're about to start."

"Yes, I was getting ready to talk to Aaron about my schedule, but he sprung this on me." Janet looked at Katie. "You didn't suggest me for the job, did you?"

"Me?" Katie placed a hand to her chest. "No, I wouldn't do that without asking you first."

Janet nodded. "I didn't really think so. I'm sorry to have asked. Only corporate could think up something like that."

"No problem." Katie shook her head but chuckled.

"I'd like to help, you know. I could help for a little while, maybe a week or two, but—"

Katie interrupted. "No, don't do it, Janet. Once you tell corporate that, they'll forget all about finding a replacement, and you'll be stuck staying the whole three months. They'll have to find someone else for us."

"You're right. Forget I said anything. It's hard enough to be away each week as it is. I can't imagine being away three months. I'd miss Gail terribly."

Katie smiled. "You've fallen for her."

"Yes." Janet grinned.

"That's wonderful. I'm happy for you."

"Thanks. I can't wait to get back to her."

"Are you going to see your parents while you're here?"

"No. I don't think I can manage that this trip. Maybe some other time."

Katie just nodded. She knew their views.

"The only thing left to do today is send Aaron my resignation as Western Regional Account Manager. I hadn't planned to quit my day job just yet, but he has forced my hand with this three-month assignment over here." Janet was more than a little nervous at the idea of quitting her job, however unpleasant her job may be, to venture into the unknown, but the decision felt right.

"You should talk to him first," Katie said.

Janet paused, deliberating. She didn't really want to talk to Aaron. He would only wheedle and cajole and try to convince her to stay, and she wasn't going to be talked into staying. Her mind was made up. She just wanted to email him her resignation and be done with him and move on to new things.

Katie was watching her and before Janet knew it, her friend had picked up the phone, dialed, and handed it to her. "At least see what your options are. You're still going to need income while your home baking business gets off the ground."

Janet took a breath. Katie was right. She should talk to Aaron and see what her options were. She accepted the phone from Katie.

As Janet exited Fulton Hospital and walked to her car, her cell phone began to buzz with notifications. She remembered that cell service was spotty in the administrative offices. One notification was a missed call from Gail but no voice mail. Janet debated calling back but needed to get to the Boston airport, so she texted to save time.

CHAPTER NINETEEN

Janet smiled as the flashing neon sign of The Pink Stallion came into view as Gail pulled into the parking lot. She felt a sudden kinship with that horse rearing up on its hind legs, as if they had both broken free of something. She had given Aaron her resignation, and they had talked, cordially enough. A weight had been lifted from her.

"You look so happy," Gail said, smiling at her.

"I am." A laugh of joy escaped Janet's lips. She was hopeful in starting her new business and hopeful in her future with the woman she loved. And she was about to go dancing. Janet was right where she wanted to be at this moment.

"Good, you deserve to be happy," Gail said as she pulled the truck into a parking space. "And I'm so happy to share it with you. For a moment, from those couple of vague phone messages of yours, I almost thought I wouldn't get to. But I don't think like that anymore, and it's because of the love you share with me."

"Oh, Gail." Janet felt moisture gather in her eyes and reached to hug Gail. "I love you so much." She felt Gail's arms wrap around her, felt the comfort and warmth of Gail.

"I love you too. And I love having you in my arms."

Janet snuggled closer.

"If we weren't meeting our friends, I think I could just stay here and hold you all evening," Gail said.

"Yes, we'd better go meet Tina and Susan before I take you up on that."

"Don't tempt me. Have I told you how hot you look tonight?" She eyed Janet's blouse.

Janet smiled. She'd chosen this new sheer plaid short-sleeved blouse knowing that the thin fabric would allow Gail to see the faint outline of her bra. The blouse was having its desired effect.

Gail shook her head and ran a hand through her short brown hair. She cast one last look at Janet's chest before getting out of the truck. She rounded the vehicle, opened Janet's door, and escorted her into The Pink Stallion.

The bar was crowded, and the dance floor was filling. Janet scanned the crowd with Gail, looking for Tina and Susan. "There they are!" Janet pointed to one of the tables across the room.

Gail placed an arm around Janet's waist and led her through the crowd. Tina and Susan greeted them with warm hugs, and they all began chatting over the music.

Janet felt a tap on her shoulder. She turned around to find a smiling Natalie and a smiling Ana. "Natalie! Ana! Hi!" Janet hugged them. "What are you doing here?" she asked with an excited smile.

"Gail invited us," Natalie said.

Janet looked at Gail in pleased wonder. "You did?" Gail had done that for her, invited Natalie?

"Yes." Gail smiled. "I found Natalie's number online and called her and Ana to join us tonight. I thought it would be a nice surprise and fun for everyone to meet each other."

Janet hugged Gail. "Thank you so much."

"You're welcome." Gail gave her a kiss.

Janet turned to look at their friends. "With everyone here, it feels like a celebration."

Gail put her arm around Janet. "We do have starting your own business to celebrate."

The group looked at Janet. "You did it? You started your own business?" Susan asked.

Janet nodded proudly. "Yes, I did. I took the leap this week."

A chorus of cheers and congratulations went up around her.

"Thanks." Janet grinned. "I'm calling it 'Grandma Cathy's,' after my grandma."

Her friends nodded and murmured approvingly. "Are you going to have much time to bake?" Ana asked.

"That's the other thing: I quit my job!" Janet could barely restrain herself from jumping for joy.

Her friends let loose with cheers and clapping, and Janet couldn't help joining in.

When the cheering quieted, Janet continued. "No more regional management for me!" Janet made a sweeping motion with her hand. "I had a long conversation with my boss. It was actually more of a heart-to-heart than I thought possible."

"What did he say?" Susan asked.

"Well, he wasn't pleased, of course. He wanted me to stay, but I don't think he realized how unhappy I was. He agreed to help me get a different position in the area here, one where I won't have to travel. I've been with the company a long time, and they don't want to lose someone like me."

"So you're going to keep working for them?" Tina asked.

"Yeah. I think I need to keep my day job until my business takes off. But I'm going to try for something part-time so that I have time to bake."

"Let me know if I can help out with tasting any of your products for you," Tina said.

The others laughed and voiced their willingness to help too.

"Watch out, I might take all of you up on it," Janet said.

The DJ announced the next dance as the Cowboy Charleston.

"If we're celebrating, then we better dance!" Susan said, with a look to encompass everyone in their group. She grabbed Tina's hand and headed for the dance floor, calling "Come on!" over her shoulder. Natalie and Ana followed. Gail turned to Janet and offered her hand. "Shall we?"

"Definitely." Janet put her hand in Gail's, and Gail led her to the dance floor.

Janet danced in the line behind Gail. The position suited her just fine. Gail looked more than a little appealing tonight, with her toned arms revealed in her sleeveless western shirt in blue and light gray plaid, tucked into her belted black jeans. Janet found that one of the nicest things about having taken dance lessons was that it left her plenty of time to admire Gail's body. The dance steps came more naturally so that she no longer had to think about them as much and could focus her attention elsewhere. She watched Gail's hips move as she stepped out and back and side to side and as she swiveled on the balls of her feet to swing out her heels. She watched Gail's arms flex as she did the dance's side-to-side pushing movements with her hands. Too soon for Janet, the dance ended.

More people entered the dance floor at a change of song, and Janet found herself with Natalie and Gail on either side of her for the next dance. It wasn't a dance that she knew, but she watched the others and picked up more steps with each repetition. She gave Natalie a smile, and Natalie gave her a proud smile back.

As Gail danced next to Janet, she admired Janet's increased style and skill on the dance floor. Natalie had obviously been a good teacher. Gail had noticed Janet and Natalie exchanging smiles. Gail was surprised to find herself feeling only happiness, not worry, over their interactions. She wouldn't have thought it possible, but memories of Christine were finally fading. Gail felt free and joyous, just like Janet looked. When Janet glanced over at her with a big smile on her face, Gail's heart ballooned with love.

Later, after much more dancing, Gail drew Janet close and said over the music, "It's getting late. Should we leave?"

Janet put her arms around Gail's neck and gazed at her. "Let's keep dancing. It just so happens that I don't have to fly anywhere tomorrow."

Bella Books, Inc.

Women. Books. Even Better Together.

P.O. Box 10543
Tallahassee, FL 32302

Phone: 800-729-4992
www.bellabooks.com